最仿真的考題 ✕ 最專業的解析
7天搞定最困難的多益題型
絕對不是不可能！

User's Guide 使用說明

7天征服多益聽力不是不可能！只要跟著以下這五大密技，你就可以輕鬆拿下最困難的對話題型！

密技 1
聽聽達人怎麼講！
金色證書高手親授應考訣竅

　　開始練考題前，一定要先知道出題方式和解題撇步，就像上場打仗前一定要先盡可能摸清敵人的底細，才能擬定出無往不利的有效策略。那麼，那些拿了金色證書的達人們，他們在考場上都是如何破題的？我們又要如何像他們一樣厲害呢？就來一探究竟吧！

金色證書高手張辰安、汪瑩瑩教你
聽力搶分小撇步

　　考聽力的其中一些題型時，題目會是「念出來」的，一聽到正確的答案，大家會立刻劃記在答案卷上。因此，有經驗的考生會建議你一個偷吃步：班上瑋論上「會寫」的人會比「不會寫」的人多，會的人一聽到正確答案就會趕快畫卡了，所以如果聽到某個選項被念出來時，整個考場大家都馬上低頭畫卡，你就知道這是正確答案，也可以跟著畫。這個方法當然有點作弊，不過用好就好了，當然，挑選跟隨的目標時要小心，不要找到一個看起來很行的人就一路跟著他畫卡，還是要「廣泛參考」以免弄錯人。

　　不拿的是，在本書專攻的「對話題型」中沒有辦法使用這一招，因為這個選項不會念出來，而是寫在題本上面。對付對話題型時，有哪些小撇步？我們詢問了許多高分的朋友，整理出一些心得，與大家分享：

搶分撇步1. 把握題型說明的時間，先把題目都掃過一遍，原到重點

　　在對話開始播放前，會先有一段答題說明，告訴你怎麼答題。基本上只要之前有看過題型，就已經知道這怎麼答了，根本不需要仔細再聽一遍說明。所以就趁這個機會先掃過題目一遍，抓到題目要問的重點。此外，聽題號其實也會花一點時間，也可以拿這個時間來抓重點。

　　至於要抓哪些重點？首先可以注意題目在問什麼（以便對話開始時，能迅速找到答案），也可以注意題目中有沒有問到需要「背起來」的東西，例如日期、時間、數字、歷年等。如果有問到這些，在對話中出現時就可以特別注意起起來：如果是沒有問到這些，你就知道就算兩人對話中講到一堆數字，你也不需要慌慌張張地去記，因為反正不會考。聽力測驗時間緊湊，能不花時間去記一些有的沒的，就盡量不要花。

010

Content 目錄

密技 2
練練考題如何寫！
60大全真模擬試題一次搞定

　　熟悉了應考訣竅，再來就是進入實戰練習！充足的考題讓應試者可以一練再練，不管是聽到不熟悉的口音就驚慌失措、還是聽到不懂的單字就煩悶挫折、或是聽到太長的對話就恍神失焦，經過全真模擬試題的磨練後，在考場上都能立刻抓住對話中的重點，直接攻克考題！

密技 3 看看原文說什麼！聽力考題文本全收錄

做完練習後，只是對完答案是沒有用的，瞭解一下原來的對話內容，找出問題所在才能加以補強。此外，一定要搭配外師親錄的MP3，多聽幾次，熟悉語速和用法，實際考試時就決不會再犯同樣的錯誤喔！

多益聽力搶分有祕密，全真模擬試題1

1. What is true about the two speakers?
(A) They work in the same office.
(B) They usually work from 8 a.m. to 5 p.m.
(C) They are brother and sister.
(D) They will go shopping together.

2. When and where will they meet after work?
(A) 7 o'clock, at the shoe store.
(B) 7:05, at Yumiko's office.
(C) 7:05, at the shoe store.
(D) 7 o'clock, at Yumiko's office.

3. What is not true about the woman?
(A) She seems to be a busy person.
(B) Making presentation slides is part of her job.
(C) She agreed to go shopping with her friend.
(D) She doesn't have a lot of work to do.

GO ON TO THE NEXT PAGE

015

密技 4 找找重點在哪裡！男女國籍口音大不同

大部分應試者覺得對話題型很難，都是因為說話者的口音常常是英、美、澳三國混在考題中的，即因此本書特別抓出搶分重點，告訴讀者哪些字是三種腔調唸起來都不一樣、什麼時候會連音、怎麼判斷說話語調，這樣一來，絕對不再怕聽不懂外籍人士的英語！

密技 5 想想關鍵怎麼破解！短短十秒搶分密招

60個題組中，每一小題都有專業的滿分高手詳解，告訴讀者要如何只要看題目就可以推論出解答、如何避開錯誤選項。如果覺得詳解太落落長，那就花十秒瞭解畫線處的關鍵吧！記住精華中的精華，一樣可以速速破解考題！

多益聽力搶分有祕密，全真模擬試題-P015頁答案與詳解

題目解答
1. (D)　　　　2. (B)　　　　3. (D)

聽力原文
M: Hey, Yumiko, are you free after work? I need to get a pair of new shoes. I can't go to my sister's wedding in these.
W: Sure, I'll come with you. I have to finish making presentation slides first though. Can you wait for me until 7?
M: No problem. I'll come by your office at around 7:05. Is that okay with you?
W: Sounds good. Oh, wow, it's 1 already? I have to get back to work. See you then!

搶分重點　◆ 口音為英澳（男）與美籍（女）。
◆ 請注意，can't這個字的英式念法和美式念法不同！

聽力中譯
M: 佑美子，妳下班後有空嗎？我得買一雙新鞋。我不可能穿我現在這雙去我姐姐的婚禮。

聽力題目詳解
1. 關於兩名說話者，何者為真？
(A) 他們在同一個辦公室工作。
(B) 他們通常會從早上八點工作到下午五點。
(C) 他們是兄妹／姊弟。
(D) 他們會一起去購物。

多益聽力搶分有祕密：滿分高手10秒解題關鍵
男子在對話中說他下班後要到佑美子的辦公室等她，可見他們兩人並非在同一個辦公室工作。對話中有提到兩人工作的時間與是否為親戚，倒是可以看出兩人下班後要一起去逛街，因此選(D)。

2. 他們下班後什麼時候、在哪裡見面？
(A) 7點在鞋店。
(B) 7:05在佑美子的辦公室。
(C) 7:05在鞋店。
(D) 7點在佑美子的辦公室。

根據統計，在「新鮮人最想進入的前百大企業」中，有超過40%的公司，都希望其員工必須具備一定的英語能力，一般來說，企業大部分會要求新進人員至少要有多益550分的程度，而大公司的採購、工程師或管理人員，都至少要具備多益750到800分的英文能力。所以眾多上班族和應屆畢業生紛紛報考多益測驗，這些現象，從年年激增的報考人數就可以看出。

除了因為「多益是商用英語，企業最愛看、在職場上最受用」之外，多益「一般不考說和寫，而且只有單選題，最好考」、「題目不會太刁鑽、最好準備」也是大家趨之若鶩的原因。但事實真的是如此嗎？想在多益拿下高分，就必須在兩小時內飆完聽力和閱讀各一百題選擇題，甚至還要有時間檢查答案，而且還不能再題目本上做記號、只能用頭腦記住文意，等於是沒有時間多做思考、推論，必須當機立斷決定答案。

閱讀一向是台灣的英語學習者的強項，從小接受的英語教育讓台灣人超會背單字、超會分析文法，因此多益閱讀並不是什麼大問題。可是一旦碰到聽力，尤其是內容又臭又長、最難抓重點的第三大題「對話題型」，許多人就只能愣在那裡，雙眼放空、腦袋恍神，像零件脫落的機器人一樣。

其實，多益的聽力測驗內容並不艱深，就算是對話題型也一樣，它是在比考生們誰的耳朵比較厲害、誰比較有耐心。多益聽力

試題只會播放一次，所以「一聽定生死」，而眾多考生往往在「語速和口音」就被打敗了。不管曾經背過多深奧的單字，題目讀得再怎麼清楚，只要耳朵跟不上說話速度、不熟悉英國腔和澳洲腔，就會導致聽不懂對話內容，讓一切付諸流水。再來，在時間的壓迫下，要怎麼樣沉住氣，冷靜聽完整段話，在聆聽的同時找出對應的選項，這也是非常重要的。

　　所以，本書專攻最讓大家害怕的對話題型，精選60組題目，讓已經準備得差不多，只是擔心在考場上碰到難以預料的狀況的學習者，只要花七天密集練習，就可以讓自己的耳朵適應各種口音、習慣語速；但如果是都還沒開始準備的考生，也用不著擔心，本書除了有對話的原文文本之外，還有對話和題目的翻譯，而且每一題都有詳細的解析，只要扎實的練習，一樣可以掌握這類題型、征服新多益。

　　最後，非常感謝捷徑編輯團隊的辰安和瑩瑩，貼心地分享她們獲得金色證書的秘訣，讓眾多徬徨的考生能更了解、注意的一些應試的眉眉角角。最後，祝福考生們能獲得滿意的成績，更由衷祝福各位能用完美的多益成績，抓住理想的工作。

Content 目錄

金色證書高手張辰安、汪瑩瑩教你 聽力搶分小撇步

考聽力的其中一些題型時，題目會是「念出來」的，一聽到正確的答案，大家會立刻畫在答案卷上。因此，有經驗的考生會建議你一個偷吃步：班上理論上「會寫」的人會比「不會寫」的人多，會的人一聽到正確答案就會趕快畫卡了，所以如果聽到某個選項被念出來時，整個考場大家都馬上低頭畫卡，你就知道這是正確答案，也可以跟著畫。這個方法當然有點作弊，不過好用就好。當然，挑選跟隨的目標時要小心，不要找到一個看起來很行的人就一路跟著他畫卡，還是要「廣泛參考」以免跟錯人。

不幸的是，在本書專攻的「對話題型」中沒有辦法使用這一招，因為每個選項不會念出來，而是寫在題本上面。對付對話題型時，有哪些小撇步？我們詢問了許多高分的朋友，整理出一些心得，與大家分享：

搶分撇步1. 把握題型說明的時間，先把題目都掃過一遍，抓到重點！

在對話開始播放前，會先有一段答題說明，告訴你怎麼答題。基本上只要之前有看過題型，就已經知道怎麼答了，根本不需要仔細再聽一遍說明，所以就趁這個機會先掃過題目一遍，抓到題目要問的重點。此外，唸題號其實也會花一點時間，也可以拿這個時間來抓重點。

至於要抓哪些重點？首先可以注意題目在問什麼（以便對話開始時，能迅速找到答案）、也可以注意題目中有沒有問到需要「背起來」的東西，例如日期、時間、數字、顏色等。如果有問到這些，在對話中出現時就可以特別注意記起來；如果並沒有問到這些，你就知道就算兩人對話中講到一堆數字，你也不需要慌慌張張地去記，因為反正不會考。聽力測驗時間緊湊，能不花時間去記一些有的沒的，就盡量不要花。

搶分撇步2. 聽到陌生的專有名詞時別緊張！根據上下文判斷就好！

我們在課本上熟悉的英文名字不外乎Mary、John那幾個，地名也不外乎London、New York那幾個。但多益走國際化路線，所以除了這些對我們來說平易近人的名字，還不時地會冒出一些日本人、印度人等等的名字，讓你措手不及，甚至誤以為是個沒背過的生字而嚇一跳。同樣地，還會偶爾跑出一些你沒聽過的地名、公司名，讓你一下不知如何是好。

如何面對這些你不可能準備到的專有名詞呢？其實不用害怕，出題老師不會那麼壞，丟給你一個陌生的城市名字考你地理。對於這些名詞，只要能根據上下文判斷它們是「人名」、「地名」、「公司名」，知道它們在對話中扮演什麼角色即可，不用特別去考慮它們的意思或背景。

搶分撇步3. 注意題號順序，一題錯題題錯，別失足成千古恨！

翻到下一頁時，先看題號順序。這是因為對話題型的題組是三個為一組，一頁可以放好幾組，而一組的對話講完後，接下來是往右邊看下一組還是往下看下一組呢？這就必須先確認，我們就有幾個朋友因為看錯題組，看到的題目與聽到的對話對不起來，整個題組的分數就白白失掉了。

搶分撇步4. 觀察題目中的「矛盾選項」，二選一，答對率更高！

如果有時間先看一下題目，發現四個選項中有衝突的選項（如：(A)彼得還未婚、(D)彼得已婚），可以猜到答案很可能就在這兩個選項之中，心裡有個底後，聽對話時就更好抓重點（例如這一題中，就要認真聽彼得到底結婚了沒）。

搶分撇步5. 找到選項中的「不合群者」做刪去法！提高答對率！

找到「和別人不一樣的選項」也是一招，例如四個選項中有三個都在講「水果」，只有一個在講「花」，你只要一聽對話的主題，應該很快就知道要馬上刪掉這個選項不管，還是直接決定選這個選項了。

搶分撇步6. 瞭解對話情境，比聽懂每個單字還重要！

在聽對話時可以想像對話的情境，並想像兩人之間的關係。別認為「對話說得這麼快，我哪有空在那邊妄想」，其實瞭解對話的情境、對話中男女的關係、並抓到對話的主旨，對做選擇題非常有幫助。

搶分撇步7. 別小看好像不重要的對話句子，那可能就是這題的關鍵！

新多益聽力測驗的對話中，兩人常會講著講著就若無其事穿插一些無關緊要的句子，例如兩人可能在面試，卻不知道為什麼聊到和人事部的誰是高中同學。但別聽到好像和主旨無關的句子就忽略它！再怎麼無關緊要的句子，題目裡還是有可能出現，所以考聽力時皮時時刻刻都要繃緊。

搶分撇步8. 利用關鍵單字做聯想，而非瞎聽瞎猜！

別讓考前背單字的努力白費！考聽力時，就要練習抓關鍵字、關鍵句。有些單字只會出現在某些地方，例如我們聽到「點菜」立刻會想到這裡是「餐廳」，聽到問「住幾晚」，就知道十之八九是「旅館」。

搶分撇步9. 魔鬼藏在細節中！小地方更要小心聽！

單複數、時態這些小地方都有可能入題，如果可以的話，盡量聽清楚錄音老師說的事情是現在還是過去發生的、是一個還是很多個。

搶分撇步10. 不會寫也別猶豫，快把心思放在下一題！

不要猶豫一些非100%確定的選項，只需要考慮100%確定的選項。聽力測驗的時間短暫，沒有時間給你懷疑。同樣的，也不需要在不會的題目上花太久的時間，真的不會就猜，反正不扣分。不要都在唸下一題了還在懊惱地回想前一題，每一題都要百分之百專注地聽，就算把腦細胞移一點點去想前一題也不行！

總歸來說，就是「聽力測驗很趕，不要浪費任何時間和精神做不需要的事，全神貫注地聽」！進考場時，請一定要牢記這一句，之前努力準備才不會全都白費喔！祝你好運！

新多益聽力
對話題型模擬試題

Directions: You will hear some conversations between two people. You will be asked to answer three questions about what the speakers say in each conversation. Select the best response to each question and mark the letter (A), (B), (C), or (D) on your answer sheet. The conversations will be spoken only one time and will not be printed in your test book.

多益聽力搶分有祕密，全真模擬試題1

1. What is true about the two speakers?　　🎧 **Track 01**

　(A) They work in the same office.

　(B) They usually work from 8 a.m. to 5 p.m.

　(C) They are brother and sister.

　(D) They will go shopping together.

2. When and where will they meet after work?

　(A) 7 o'clock, at the shoe store.

　(B) 7:05, at Yumiko's office.

　(C) 7:05, at the shoe store.

　(D) 7 o'clock, at Yumiko's office.

3. What is not true about the woman?

　(A) She seems to be a busy person.

　(B) Making presentation slides is part of her job.

　(C) She agreed to go shopping with her friend.

　(D) She doesn't have a lot of work to do.

GO ON TO THE NEXT PAGE ➤

題目解答

1. (D)   2. (B)   3. (D)

聽力原文

M: Hey, Yumiko, are you free after work? I need to get a pair of new shoes. I can't^英 go to my sister's wedding in these.

W: Sure, I'll come with you. I have to finish making presentation slides first though. Can you wait for me until 7?

M: No problem. I'll come by your office at around 7:05. Is that okay with you?

W: Sounds good. Oh, wow, it's 1 already? I have to get back to work. See you then!

> **搶分重點**
> ❶ 口音為英國（男）與美國（女）。
> ❷ 請注意，can't 這個字的英式念法和美式念法不同！

聽力中譯

M： 佑美子，妳下班後有空嗎？我得買一雙新鞋。我不可能穿我現在這雙去我姐姐的婚禮。

W： 好啊，我跟你去。不過我要先做好簡報投影片，妳可以等我到七點嗎？

M： 沒問題，我在7:05左右到妳辦公室，可以嗎？

W： 聽起來很好啊。 喔，哇，已經一點了喔？我得回去工作了，到時候見！

聽力題目詳解

1. 關於兩名說話者，何者為真？

(A) 他們在同一個辦公室工作。

(B) 他們通常會從早上八點工作到下午五點。

(C) 他們是兄妹／姊弟。

(D) 他們會一起去購物。

多益聽力搶分有祕密，滿分高手10秒解題關鍵

男子在對話中說他下班後要到佑美子的辦公室等她，可見他們兩人並非在同一個辦公室工作。對話中並未提到兩人工作的時間與是否為親戚，倒是可以聽出兩人下班後要一起去逛街，因此選(D)。

2. 他們下班後什麼時候、在哪裡見面？

(A) 7點在鞋店。

(B) 7:05在佑美子的辦公室。

(C) 7:05在鞋店。

(D) 7點在佑美子的辦公室。

多益聽力搶分有祕密，滿分高手10秒解題關鍵

如果有時間先將題目掃過一遍，抓到「When」和「Where」兩個關鍵字，便可以在聽對話時仔細聽所有的時間和地點。別被一些「七點」、「一點」的時間給干擾了喔！

3. 關於女子，何者不為真？

(A) 她感覺是個挺忙碌的人。

(B) 做簡報投影片是她工作的一部分。

(C) 她同意和她朋友去購物。

(D) 她沒有很多工作要做。

多益聽力搶分有祕密，滿分高手10秒解題關鍵

將題目迅速看過一遍，很快可以發現(A)和(D)兩個選項的內容幾乎可以說是互相衝突的，可以大概猜到正確答案八九不離十地是在這兩項裡面。於是，聽對話時，只要仔細注意佑美子到底忙不忙，就能夠回答這一題了喔！

多益聽力搶分有祕密，全真模擬試題2

1. What is true about the GX-223?　　　🎧 **Track 02**

(A) It is a type of microwave.

(B) It comes with a manual.

(C) It is currently on discount.

(D) It comes with a 1-month guarantee.

2. What kind of machine does the woman like best?

(A) The kind that runs smoothly.

(B) The kind that comes with a manual.

(C) The kind that is light and easy to use.

(D) The kind with a pretty color.

3. What machine did the woman end up buying?

(A) The GX-223.

(B) The AX-012.

(C) Both of them.

(D) Neither of them.

GO ON TO THE NEXT PAGE ➤

題目解答

1. **(B)**　　　　　2. **(D)**　　　　　3. **(D)**

聽力原文

M: Good morning. How may I help you, Miss?

W: I'm looking for a lawnmower. Is there any discount right now?

M: Here are some of our newest models英. The GX-223 right here is very popular. It comes with a handy manual and a 1-year guarantee! Also, I personally recommend the AX-012. It works like a dream and is on discount this week.

W: Nah, the color looks ugly. I'll take this hot pink one.

> **搶分重點**
> ❷ 口音為英國（男）與美國（女）。
> ❷ 我們中文常把model叫做「麻豆」，這是因為美國腔中，model的念法有點像「媽斗」。但英國腔中聽起來卻不是如此，有沒有注意到呢？

聽力中譯

M：早安，我可以幫妳什麼嗎，小姐？

W：我在找割草機。現在有在打折的嗎？

M：這裡有一些新的機型。這台GX-223很受歡迎，還附好用的手冊與一年的保固！我個人還很推薦AX-012，超級好用，而且本週特價。

W：不要啦，顏色好醜。我要買這台亮粉紅色的。

聽力題目詳解

1. 關於GX-223，何者為真？

(A) 是一種微波爐。

(B) 有附手冊。

(C) 現在在打折。

(D) 有一個月的保固。

多益聽力搶分有祕密，滿分高手10秒解題關鍵

對話中提到兩種不同機型的割草機，這時就要仔細聽並快速地在腦中記下（多益不能在題本上做筆記）兩種機型各自的特色，且不能混淆。在這裡我們知道有打折的是AX-012，而題目中所問的GX-223並沒有打折，再加上GX-223的保固期並非一個月，且不是一種微波爐，所以就只能選(B)了。

2. 這位女子最喜歡哪種機器？

(A) 運作順暢的機器。

(B) 有附手冊的機器。

(C) 輕便又容易使用的機器。

(D) 顏色漂亮的機器。

多益聽力搶分有祕密，滿分高手10秒解題關鍵

對話中，店員向女子介紹了不同機型的好處，但她最後還是獨鍾亮粉紅色的機器，可見對她而言，顏色漂亮才是選擇機器的重點。

3. 女子最後買了哪種機器？

(A) 買了GX-223。

(B) 買了AX-012。

(C) 兩台都買了。

(D) 兩台都沒有買。

多益聽力搶分有祕密，滿分高手10秒解題關鍵

雖然售貨員介紹的兩種機型都有許多優點，但女子嫌棄它們顏色難看，可見她最後並沒有挑選這些機型，兩台都沒有買。

多益聽力搶分有祕密，全真模擬試題3

1. What can we infer from the conversation?　　🎧 **Track 03**

   (A) It is not currently winter.

   (B) The woman has no friends.

   (C) You get a discount of 50% if you buy three down jackets.

   (D) The woman bought one down jacket in the end.

2. If the woman bought one down jacket, how much would she have to pay?

   (A) 200 dollars.

   (B) 150 dollars.

   (C) 100 dollars.

   (D) 50 dollars.

3. What did the woman end up buying?

   (A) Two black down jackets.

   (B) Two down jackets, one yellow and one blue.

   (C) Two down jackets, one yellow and one black.

   (D) One blue down jacket.

GO ON TO THE NEXT PAGE ➤

題目解答

1. **(A)**   2. **(B)**   3. **(C)**

聽力原文

W: How much is this down jacket?

M: We're having an off-season promotion right now. It normally costs 200 Dollars, but is 150 now. Also, you get a special discount of 50% if you get two! Why don't you consider it?

W: Um, why would I want two? One down jacket is quite enough.

M: You can buy one for yourself, and give the other to a friend.

W: Makes sense. Okay, I'll take this yellow one and that black one.

搶分重點 🔊 口音為英國（男）與美國（女）。

聽力中譯

W： 這件羽絨外套多少錢？

M： 我們現在在進行淡季促銷的活動。這件平常要200元，但現在只要150。如果買兩件，還特價五折！要不要考慮一下啊？

W： 呃，可是我要兩件幹嘛？一件羽絨外套就很夠了吧。

M： 妳可以買一件自己穿，一件給朋友啊。

W： 有理耶。好，那我買這件黃的跟那件黑的。

聽力題目詳解

1. 我們從這個對話可以得知什麼訊息？

　　(A) 現在不是冬天。

　　(B) 女人沒有朋友。

　　(C) 如果買三件羽絨外套可打五折。

　　(D) 女人最後買了一件羽絨外套。

多益聽力搶分有祕密，滿分高手10秒解題關鍵

由「淡季促銷」（off-season promotion）這個關鍵字，可以得知現在不是適合穿羽絨衣的季節，所以不是冬天，要選(A)。這種需要一點推理的題目比較困難，也可以利用刪去法，判斷不是其他三個選項而選出正確的答案。

2. 如果女人買了一件羽絨外套，那她應該付多少錢？

　　(A) 200元。

　　(B) 150 元。

　　(C) 100元。

　　(D) 50元。

多益聽力搶分有祕密，滿分高手10秒解題關鍵

對話中，店員提到「一件羽絨衣平常要200元，但現在只要150元」，可知買一件需付150元，別被買兩件時的特價給搞昏頭了。

3. 女人最後買了什麼呢？

   (A) 兩件黑色的羽絨外套。

   (B) 一件黃色、一件藍色的羽絨外套。

   (C) 一件黃色、一件黑色的羽絨外套。

   (D) 一件藍色的羽絨外套。

多益聽力搶分有祕密，滿分高手10秒解題關鍵

在快速掃過題目一遍時，注意到有和顏色有關的選項，在聽對話時就更要仔細注意有出現顏色的地方。可以快速地運用想像力，如果一聽到「黃色和黑色」，腦中就立刻出現黃色和黑色的物體（如蜜蜂），可以記得比較清楚。

多益聽力搶分有祕密，全真模擬試題4

1. What can we infer from the conversation?　　🎧 **Track 04**

   (A) The man wants a new smartphone.

   (B) The woman offers to fix the phone herself.

   (C) The man will receive his phone in 7 days.

   (D) The man and the woman are in a phone factory.

2. What is wrong with the man's phone?

   (A) It cannot be plugged in.

   (B) It is charging, but doesn't look like it.

   (C) It looks like it is charging, but isn't.

   (D) Its screen needs to be fixed.

3. Why does the man request that his phone is sent to his company?

   (A) He has no mailbox at home.

   (B) He lives in his company.

   (C) The phone belongs to his boss.

   (D) He wants his coworkers to see his new phone.

GO ON TO THE NEXT PAGE

多益聽力搶分有祕密，
全真模擬試題-P027頁答案與詳解

題目解答

1. (C)　　　　　　2. (C)　　　　　　3. (A)

聽力原文

M: My smartphone is no longer chargeable. Can you fix this for me?

W: Wait, what do you mean by no longer chargeable?

M: I plugged it in, it looked as if it were charging—but it wasn't!

W: I see. We'll send it back to the factory for a check and deliver it back to you in ②7 days.

M: Sure, just let me write down my company address. I don't have a mailbox at home, so you'll have to send it to where I work.

> **搶分重點**
> ❶ 口音為英國（男）與美國（女）。
> ❷ 注意到這裡的「in」和「7 days」之間小小停頓了一下嗎？這表示說話的人在思考，在這裡我們可以推測女子是因為在計算男子的手機修好的天數而停下來思考。

聽力中譯

M： 我的智慧型手機不能充電了，妳可以幫我修嗎？

W： 等等，你說不能充電了是什麼意思？

M： 我插了電以後，看起來好像有在充電，但其實沒有在充。

W： 我懂了。我們會把它送回工廠檢查，並在七天內送回給你。

M：好啊，讓我寫下我公司的地址。我家沒信箱，所以妳得寄到我
工作的地方。

聽力題目詳解

1. 我們可以從以上對話得知什麼？

(A) 這名男子想要新的智慧型手機。

(B) 女子主動說要親自修手機。

(C) 男子會在七天內收到手機。

(D) 男子與女子在一家手機工廠中。

多益聽力搶分有祕密，滿分高手10秒解題關鍵

(A) 男子是將他的手機送修，而不是想要新的。(B) 女子說要將手
機送去工廠，而不是她自己修。(D) 女子說要將手機送去工廠，可
見他們兩人現在並不在工廠，不然不需要「送」這個步驟。因此，
該選擇(C)。

---

2. 男子的手機出了什麼問題？

(A) 無法插電。

(B) 看起來沒有在充電，但其實有在充。

(C) 看起來有在充電，但其實沒有在充。

(D) 螢幕需要修了。

男子手機的問題有點複雜，要仔細聽，才能確定到底是哪一個問題，尤其是(B)與(C)這種長得很像的選項，更要小心判斷。其中(D)選項可以首先刪掉，因為對話從頭到尾並未提到手機的螢幕。

3. 男子為何要求把手機寄到他的公司？

   (A) **他家裡沒有信箱。**

   (B) 他住在公司。

   (C) 手機是他老闆的。

   (D) 他要同事們看他的新手機。

有時題目中會出現似乎與正題無關，彷彿閒聊般的句子，這裡男人在修手機時若無其事地提到家裡沒信箱就是一例。聽題目時從頭到尾都要繃緊神經仔細聽，搞不好題目就藏在這種閒聊般的句子裡呢！

多益聽力搶分有祕密，全真模擬試題5

1. Where are the man and woman?　　　🎧 **Track 05**

   (A) They are in a boutique.

   (B) They are in an office.

   (C) They are in a meeting room.

   (D) They are in a restaurant.

2. For how long has the man been waiting?

   (A) Two hours.

   (B) One hour.

   (C) Half an hour.

   (D) One hour and a half.

3. Why did the man say "gotta go"?

   (A) He left his water somewhere else.

   (B) He was waiting in the wrong restaurant.

   (C) He saw his client approach.

   (D) He is frightened of the waitress.

GO ON TO THE NEXT PAGE ➤

多益聽力搶分有祕密，
全真模擬試題-P031頁答案與詳解

題目解答

1. (D)　　　　2. (A)　　　　3. (B)

聽力原文

W: Sir, would you like to order now?

M: I'm waiting for my client. We'll order together when he gets here.

W: But sir, you've been sitting here for two hours. Would you at least like some water?

M: It's been two hours already? Wow, Mr. Abu Bakar sure[2] is late. Wait, is this the Royal Green Restaurant?

W: Uh, no.

M: Oops, gotta go!

> **搶分重點**
>
> ❶ 口音為英國（男）與美國（女）。
>
> ❷ 男子在「sure」這個字加了重音，是為了強調這個字，表示「阿布巴卡先生『真是』遲到超久」，可以推測男子等得很不耐煩了。

聽力中譯

W：先生，您現在要點餐嗎？

M：我在等我的客戶。等他到了，我們再一起點。

W：但先生，您已經在這裡坐兩個小時了。要不要先來點水呢？

M：已經兩個小時了喔？哇，阿布巴卡先生真是遲到太久了。等等，這是皇家格林餐廳嗎？

W：呃，不是耶。

M：糟糕，我該走人了！

聽力題目詳解

1. 男人與女人在哪裡？

    (A) 他們在精品店裡。

    (B) 他們在辦公室裡。

    (C) 他們在會議室裡。

    (D) 他們在餐廳裡。

多益聽力搶分有祕密，滿分高手10秒解題關鍵

從對話中女子詢問男子是否要點餐，可以聽出兩人現在應該是在餐廳裡，而女子是服務生。

---

2. 男子等多久了？

    (A) 兩個小時。

    (B) 一個小時。

    (C) 半個小時。

    (D) 一小時半。

由女子所說的內容，可以判斷男子已經在那家餐廳裡坐了兩個小時。對話中並未出現其他的時間點，所以很容易能夠得知這題的答案。

3. 男子為什麼說「我該走人了」？

(A) 他把水放在別的地方了。

(B) 他等錯餐廳了。

(C) 他看到客戶來了。

(D) 他害怕服務生。

雖然對話中出現「水」（water）和「客戶」（client）的單字，但男子要離開的實際原因是發現自己所在的餐廳不是心裡想的那家，別被干擾選項給誤導了。

多益聽力搶分有祕密，全真模擬試題6

1. Who is Julie? 🎧 **Track 06**

   (A) She is the woman's sister.

   (B) She is the man's relative.

   (C) She works in the same company as the man and woman.

   (D) She is the woman's young daughter.

2. What can we infer about the woman?

   (A) She has more than one child.

   (B) She is good friends with Julie.

   (C) She is related to the man.

   (D) She likes rainy days.

3. What can we infer from the conversation?

   (A) It might be sunny on Friday.

   (B) It might rain on Saturday.

   (C) The company picnic is on Sunday.

   (D) The woman will bring her family to work on Monday.

GO ON TO THE NEXT PAGE ➤

多益聽力搶分有祕密，
全真模擬試題-P035頁答案與詳解

題目解答

1. (C)   2. (A)   3. (B)

聽力原文

W: Are you coming to the company picnic on Saturday? I'm going to bring my whole family.

M: Oh, I do plan to go if it's sunny, but according to the forecast^英 it will likely rain. Julie from accounting said they might cancel it.

W: Really? That's too bad! My kids have been looking forward to it for the whole week.

M: Well, look on the bright side! The forecast can be wrong.

> **搶分重點**
> ➊ 口音為英國（男）與美國（女）。
> ➋ 英國腔中的「forecast」，特別是「cast」的部分比較特別，可以多聽看看。

聽力中譯

W：你禮拜六要參加公司辦的野餐嗎？我要帶我全家去。

M：喔，我打算如果出太陽就會去，可是根據氣象預報所說很可能會下雨。會計部的茱麗說活動可能會取消。

W：真的喔？那太慘了，我的孩子們整個禮拜都很期待的說。

M：唉呀，要往好處想啊！氣象預報可能會不準。

聽力題目詳解

1. 茉麗是誰？

(A) 她是女子的姊妹。

(B) 她是男子的親戚。

(C) 她和男子與女子在同一個公司工作。

(D) 她是女子的小女兒。

多益聽力搶分有祕密，滿分高手10秒解題關鍵

在對話中茉麗被稱為「會計部的茉麗」（Julie from accounting），
且她似乎對公司辦的野餐相關訊息很瞭解，可知她和男子與女子是
在同一家公司工作，而非兩人的親戚。

2. 有關女子，我們可以得知什麼事？

(A) 她有超過一個孩子。

(B) 她和茉麗是好朋友。

(C) 她和男子是親戚。

(D) 她喜歡雨天。

多益聽力搶分有祕密，滿分高手10秒解題關鍵

女子在提到她的孩子們期待野餐時，用了「kids」這個複數名詞，
可知女子的孩子不只一個。在聽題目時要小心名詞的單複數，就算
是這樣的小地方也有可能成為考題的一部分。

3. 我們從對話中可得知什麼訊息？

　　(A) 星期五可能會出太陽。

　　(B) 星期六可能會下雨。

　　(C) 公司野餐是在禮拜天舉辦。

　　(D) 女子會在星期一帶她的家人去工作。

多益聽力搶分有祕密，滿分高手**10秒解題關鍵**

一下看到一大堆的「星期幾」雖然令人眼花撩亂，但只要在聽對話時抓住關鍵訊息：野餐是在星期六舉辦，選出正確答案就不困難了。

多益聽力搶分有祕密，全真模擬試題7

1. Where are the man and woman going after the conference?

   (A) To the sushi place.　　　　　　　🎧 **Track 07**

   (B) To the pizza place.

   (C) To two blocks away.

   (D) We do not know.

2. What can we infer about the man?

   (A) He had sushi a week ago.

   (B) He did not want to walk two blocks.

   (C) He likes pizza much better than sushi.

   (D) He doesn't mind sushi two days in a row.

3. What can we infer about the man and woman?

   (A) They've never eaten out together before.

   (B) They are classmates.

   (C) They have eaten pizza together before.

   (D) They have been dating for some time.

GO ON TO THE NEXT PAGE ➤

多益聽力搶分有祕密，
全真模擬試題-P039頁答案與詳解

題目解答

1. (D)　　　　　2. (D)　　　　　3. (C)

聽力原文

W: Want to 美 grab a bite together after the conference?

M: Sure. What place do you have in mind?

W: There's this new sushi place just around the corner. If you're in a pizza kind of mood, we could also walk two blocks to that pizza place we tried last time.

M: I had sushi yesterday, so I would prefer we get pizza. I don't mind sushi two days in a row if you really really want sushi though.

> **搶分重點**
> ❶ 口音為英國（男）與美國（女）。
> ❷ 在英文口語中念得快時，常會把兩個字若無其事地黏在一起，如這裡的want to兩字之間並沒有特別斷開，聽起來有點像「wanna」。

聽力中譯

W： 研討會完要一起去吃點東西嗎？

M： 好啊，妳想去哪吃？

W： 轉角那邊有個新的壽司店。如果你是想吃披薩的心情，我們也可以走兩個街區到我們上次吃的那家披薩店。

M： 我昨天就吃過壽司了，所以我比較想買披薩。不過如果妳真的真的很想要壽司，那我也不介意連吃兩天壽司。

聽力題目詳解

1. 男子與女子研討會後要去哪？

(A) 去壽司店。

(B) 去披薩店。

(C) 去兩個街區以外的地方。

(D) 我們不知道。

多益聽力搶分有祕密，滿分高手10秒解題關鍵

這題很賊，女人詢問男人的意見，男人卻說兩個都可以，到頭來我們還是不知道到底兩個人最後決定去什麼地方。如果他們再多講兩句，或許就可以推理出來了，但對話就在這裡終止，所以我們也只能選(D)「不知道」了。

---

2. 有關男子，我們可以得知什麼事？

(A) 他一個禮拜前吃了壽司。

(B) 他不想走兩個街區。

(C) 他喜歡披薩遠勝過壽司。

(D) 他不介意連續兩天吃壽司。

多益聽力搶分有祕密，滿分高手10秒解題關鍵

雖然男子說他比較想吃披薩，但這不代表他比較喜歡披薩，而不喜歡壽司。他沒有選擇吃壽司，只是因為壽司昨天已經吃過了而已。因此(C)是一個陷阱，要小心避開它！

3. 有關男子與女子，我們可以得知什麼訊息？

    (A) 他們不曾一起出去吃過飯。

    (B) 他們是同學。

    (C) 他們曾一起吃過披薩。

    (D) 他們已經約會一陣子了。

多益聽力搶分有祕密，滿分高手10秒解題關鍵

女子在對話中提到他們曾一起去過兩個街區外的那家披薩店，可知兩人曾一起吃過披薩，所以選(C)。至於(B)與(D)的選項，兩人當然有可能是同學，也有可能在約會，但我們無法從對話中判斷，因此不能選這兩個答案。

多益聽力搶分有祕密，全真模擬試題8

1. Where does the woman work?   🎧 **Track 08**

   (A) She works at a restaurant.

   (B) She works at a hotel.

   (C) She works at a museum.

   (D) She works at a school.

2. What do we know about the man's boss?

   (A) He will be staying abroad for four nights.

   (B) He will bring his wife on the trip.

   (C) He speaks French.

   (D) He is on good terms with the woman.

3. Where is Toulouse most likely located?

   (A) In Spain.

   (B) In France.

   (C) In the UK.

   (D) In India.

GO ON TO THE NEXT PAGE

多益聽力搶分有祕密，
全真模擬試題-P043頁答案與詳解

題目解答

1. (B)   2. (C)   3. (B)

聽力原文

M: Hello. I would like to book a single room for my boss, please.

W: How long will your boss be staying here?

M: For three nights, from the fifth to the eighth. He doesn't speak English, so it would be great if you have staff^英 who could speak French to help him out.

W: No worries; we have staff members who come from Toulouse. We will do our best to make sure he has a great stay.

> **搶分重點**
> ❶ 口音為英國（男）與美國（女）。
> ❷ 英國腔的「staff」發音和美國腔的完全不同，母音有點像是比較長的「ㄚ」，別和「stuff」搞混了。

聽力中譯

M： 你好，我想替我老闆訂一間單人房。

W： 你的老闆要在這裡住多久呢？

M： 三個晚上，五號到八號。他不會說英文，所以如果有會講法文的員工可以幫他，那會很棒的。

W： 不用擔心，我們有土魯斯來的員工，我們會盡力讓他此行住得愉快。

聽力題目詳解

1. 女子在哪裡工作？

(A) 她在一家餐廳工作。

(B) 她在一家旅館工作。

(C) 她在一間博物館工作。

(D) 她在一所學校工作。

多益聽力搶分有祕密，滿分高手10秒解題關鍵

由男子打電話進來訂房可得知接電話的女子應是在旅館工作，且男子的老闆要待上三晚，可判斷不會是餐廳、博物館或學校。

2. 有關男子的老闆，我們已知哪些事？

(A) 他會在國外住四晚。

(B) 他會帶太太一起出國。

(C) 他會說法文。

(D) 他和女子交情不錯。

多益聽力搶分有祕密，滿分高手10秒解題關鍵

男子提到他老闆不會說英文，需要會說法文的員工幫忙，可見老闆會說法文。別被男子在前面所提到的「英文」混淆視聽了！

3. 土魯斯很可能在哪裡？

(A) 在西班牙。

(B) 在法國。

(C) 在英國。

(D) 在印度。

多益聽力搶分有祕密，滿分高手10秒解題關鍵

新多益有時會故意在聽力的對話中放入一些我們不習慣聽到的人名、地名，因為畢竟這是一個國際化的考試，不會只以英語系國家為中心。如果突然出現像Toulouse這種你很可能沒聽過的地名，怎麼辦呢？不用急，新多益不是要考你地理，只要從對話中「男子的老闆說法文」這條線索判斷，可知從法語系國家來的員工最能提供老闆協助，所以只要從四個選項中挑出法語系國家即可（出題人員不會殘忍地放入「加拿大」來混淆視聽）。

多益聽力搶分有祕密，全真模擬試題9

1. Why did the woman call the man?　　　🎧 **Track 09**

   (A) To ask about an apartment.

   (B) To ask about an audition.

   (C) To ask him for his number.

   (D) To ask him for his full name.

2. What do we know about the man and woman?

   (A) They are colleagues.

   (B) They are going to arrange a time to meet tomorrow.

   (C) They will meet up today.

   (D) They are staying in the same apartment.

3. What do we know about the woman?

   (A) She is looking for an apartment.

   (B) She has an interview to attend.

   (C) She is not available tomorrow.

   (D) She lives close by.

GO ON TO THE NEXT PAGE ➤

題目解答

1. **(A)**　　　2. **(B)**　　　3. **(A)**

聽力原文

W: Hello. I saw an ad that said you have an apartment to let.[2] Is it still available?

M: It is, it is! Would you like to swing by and take a look? I happen to be close by right now.

W: I can't make it over now; I've got an audition later. Will you be around tomorrow?

M: Yep, just leave your name and contact info.

W: Pamela Hayes, 090-255-9595.

搶分重點

[1] 口音為英國（男）與美國（女）。

[2] 這句雖然以「.」做結，似乎不是問句，但女子的語尾上揚，似乎帶點疑問的意思。這是因為女子打電話是要確認是否有套房要出租，有點擔心自己找錯人，所以在問的時候就帶點疑問語氣。

聽力中譯

W： 你好，我看到一個廣告，說您有套房要出租，現在還有嗎？

M： 還有，還有！妳要順道過來看一下嗎？我人剛好就在附近。

W： 我現在沒辦法過去，待會要試鏡。您明天會在嗎？

M： 會啊，留下妳的名字和聯絡方式就好。

W：潘蜜拉·海斯，090-255-9595。

聽力題目詳解

1. 女子為何會打電話給男子？

　　(A) 詢問套房的事。

　　(B) 詢問試鏡的事。

　　(C) 詢問他的電話號碼。

　　(D) 詢問他的全名。

多益聽力搶分有祕密，滿分高手10秒解題關鍵

聽完這個對話，你或許會很想說：「這女的要試鏡的事跟這個對話
有什麼關連嗎？她幹嘛硬要講啊？」但就像我們平常對話本來就會
混入一些不必要的資訊，新多益的聽力測驗中也常如此。這時，判斷
什麼是對話的主線就很重要。例如在這個對話中，你需要掌握的是
女子想租房子，她試鏡的事只是一個干擾選項，這裡也不能選(B)。

---

2. 有關男子與女子，我們已知哪些資訊？

　　(A) 他們是同事。

　　(B) 他們明天要安排時間見面。

　　(C) 他們今天會見面。

　　(D) 他們住在同一間套房。

從題目中有「明天見面」和「今天見面」兩個「見面」的選項，幾乎就可以判斷正確答案應該是這兩個的其中一個，八九不離十了。這時，只要仔細聽對話，弄清楚兩人打算約什麼時間見面，就能回答這一題。

3. 有關女子，我們知道什麼資訊？

(A) 她在找套房。

(B) 她要參加面試。

(C) 她明天沒有空。

(D) 她住在附近。

整個對話的主線講的就是女子詢問套房的事，可知她正在找套房。注意(B)選項中的interview（面試）和女子要去的audition（試鏡）是不同的，audition是應徵各種演出、表演、或加入某表演相關團體等前需要經過的步驟，而interview是應徵工作、申請大學、研究所等等前經過的步驟。

多益聽力搶分有祕密，全真模擬試題10

1. What is wrong with the woman's CD?   🎧 **Track 10**

   (A) It won't play.

   (B) It does not fit in the CD player.

   (C) It is broken.

   (D) She did not receive it.

2. How will the man deal with the problem?

   (A) He will get someone to mail a CD to the woman.

   (B) He will ask the woman to buy a new one.

   (C) He will return the money to the woman.

   (D) He will give the woman a discount.

3. What do we know about the woman?

   (A) She bought a book from a bookstore.

   (B) She sent a CD to the author.

   (C) She is learning Korean.

   (D) She bought a book online.

GO ON TO THE NEXT PAGE →

多益聽力搶分有祕密，
全真模擬試題-P051頁答案與詳解

題目解答

1. (D)   2. (A)   3. (D)

聽力原文

M: How may I help you?

W: I bought one of your books online. It says ² it comes with a CD on the cover, but I don't see one anywhere.

M: I see. We'll send one to you for free, but first please give me the title of the book and the name of the author.

W: It's called *Japanese for Beginners*, and the author is Miyazaki Misa.

M: Ah, that one. No problem, we have some spare CDs available. I'll get someone to mail a copy to you as soon as possible.

> **搶分重點**
> ❶ 口音為英國（男）與美國（女）。
> ❷ 「say」這個字我們會唸 [se]，所以「says」就是在後面加上一個s囉？不對！仔細聽聽，女子說的says母音比較短，這才是正確的念法。

聽力中譯

M： 我可以如何幫助您呢？

W： 我在網路上買了一本你們的書，封面上說會有CD，可是我到處都找不到啊。

M： 我瞭解了。我們會免費寄一片給您，但請先給我書名與作者名。

W：書名叫《初學者的日本語》，作者是宮崎美彩。

M：啊，那本啊。沒問題，我們有一些多的CD，我會找人盡快寄給您。

聽力題目詳解

1. 女子的光碟怎麼了？

(A) 播放不出來。

(B) 無法放入音響。

(C) 壞掉了。

(D) 她沒收到。

多益聽力搶分有祕密，滿分高手10秒解題關鍵

女子打電話去抗議的理由是「這本書應該要有CD，我卻沒有看到CD」，可見她根本沒有收到CD。既然沒有收到CD，其他的選項也就不可能發生了，因此選(D)。

2. 男子將如何處理這個問題？

(A) 他會請人寄一張光碟給女子。

(B) 他會請女子買一張新的。

(C) 他會退錢給女子。

(D) 他會給女子打折。

男子在對話中的最後一句說：他們有多餘的光碟，他會找人盡快寄一張新的光碟給女子，可知要選(A)，而非其他方式。

3. 有關女子，我們知道什麼資訊？

(A) 她在書局買了一本書。

(B) 她送了一張光碟給作者。

(C) 她在學韓文。

(D) 她在網路上買了一本書。

由(A)和(D)衝突的兩個選項，我們可以猜到答案很可能就在兩者之中。那麼女子到底是在書局買了書還是在網路上買了書？她第一句就把答案說出來了，因此我們可以信心滿滿地選(D)。

多益聽力搶分有祕密，全真模擬試題11

1. What do we know about the man and woman?　🎧 **Track 11**

(A) They're classmates.

(B) They're colleagues.

(C) They're married.

(D) They're father and daughter.

2. Where will the company move to?

(A) It will move to Cockfosters.

(B) It will move to space.

(C) We do not know.

(D) It will not move.

3. Why does the woman talk about resigning?

(A) She is tired of all the new recruits.

(B) Commuting may be a problem for her.

(C) She is moving to another building.

(D) She is somewhere in the Cockfosters area.

GO ON TO THE NEXT PAGE

多益聽力搶分有祕密，全真模擬試題-P055頁答案與詳解

題目解答

1. **(B)**　　　　　　2. **(C)**　　　　　　3. **(B)**

聽力原文

M: Did you hear? We might be moving to new quarters at the end of the year.

W: What? Where to?

M: Not sure, but probably some place bigger. We're running out of space to fit in all our new recruits. The company can afford to rent a larger building, I think.

W: If we move to somewhere in the Cockfosters area though, I'll have to resign. Commuting will be a huge problem for me.

搶分重點　🔊 口音為英國（男）與美國（女）。

聽力中譯

M： 妳有聽說嗎？我們年底可能要搬到新的地方。

W： 啊？搬去哪？

M： 不確定耶，不過應該會是比較大的地方吧。我們已經沒空間給新人坐了。我們公司應該租得起比較大的大樓吧，我想。

W： 不過，如果我們搬去柯克佛司特那一帶，我就得辭職了，這樣通勤會是很大的問題。

聽力題目詳解

1. 關於男子與女子，我們知道什麼訊息？

　　(A) 他們是同學。

　　(B) 他們是同事。

　　(C) 他們是夫妻。

　　(D) 他們是父女。

多益聽力搶分有祕密，滿分高手10秒解題關鍵

由男子提到「我覺得公司應該租得起更大的大樓」可知兩人討論的是公司搬遷的事宜。由對話可知兩人都在這家公司工作，所以應選「同事」最合理。雖然兩人當然也有可能是同學、夫妻與父女的關係，但從對話中無法確定，所以也不能選其他的選項。

2. 公司要搬去哪裡？

　　(A) 會搬去柯克佛司特。

　　(B) 會搬到外太空。

　　(C) 我們不知道。

　　(D) 不會搬。

多益聽力搶分有祕密，滿分高手10秒解題關鍵

對話中，男子說公司要搬遷，但他也不確定是搬去哪裡，因此我們只能選(C)。這裡的「space」指的是「外太空」，和對話中的「running out of space」的「space」指的是「空間」意思不同。

3. 女子為什麼提到辭職的事？

(A) 她受不了新人了。

(B) 通勤可能會造成她的困擾。

(C) 她要搬去另一個大樓了。

(D) 她在柯克佛司特區某處。

多益聽力搶分有祕密，滿分高手10秒解題關鍵

對話中常會出現許多干擾的字句混淆視聽，如這裡提到的「新人」
（recruits）就是。雖然新人多到公司快沒空間了，但不代表女子
受不了他們。讓她受不了的還是通勤的問題，因而選(B)。

多益聽力搶分有祕密，全真模擬試題12

1. Who is Suriya? 🎧 **Track 12**

   (A) She likely works with the man and woman.

   (B) She likely works for the man and woman.

   (C) She likely cleans up for the man and woman.

   (D) She likely lives with the man and woman.

2. What does the man want the woman to do?

   (A) To dust boxes.

   (B) To take down posters.

   (C) To greet clients.

   (D) To ask Suriya to go somewhere else.

3. Why are the man and woman cleaning?

   (A) Because their friends are coming to their house.

   (B) Because Suriya is coming to their apartment.

   (C) Because Suriya wants their posters.

   (D) Because some clients are coming over.

GO ON TO THE NEXT PAGE ➡

題目解答

1. **(A)**　　　　2. **(A)**　　　　3. **(D)**

聽力原文

M: Hey, Suriya asked[英] us to clean up this place a bit. Some clients are coming over in the afternoon.

W: What? But this office is a mess! Can't Suriya bring her clients somewhere else?

M: Nah, you know how she is. Help me move these files, and dust those boxes after you're done.

W: Okay, okay. Better take down these posters too!

搶分重點　❶ 口音為英國（男）與美國（女）。
　　　　　　❷ 英國腔的「ask」發音和美國腔不同。

聽力中譯

M：喂，蘇利亞要我們把這地方清一清。下午會有客戶過來。

W：啊？可是這辦公室超亂耶！蘇利亞不能帶她的客戶去別的地方嗎？

M：不行啊，妳也知道她的個性。幫我搬一下這些文件，搬完後再撢一下那些箱子。

W：好啦，好啦。這些海報最好也拿下來！

聽力題目詳解

1. 蘇利亞是誰？

(A) 她很可能是男子和女子的同事。

(B) 她很可能替男子和女子工作。

(C) 她很可能是替男子與女子打掃的人。

(D) 她很可能與男子和女子同住。

多益聽力搶分有祕密，滿分高手10秒解題關鍵

現在Mary之類的名字已經退流行了，使用這個名字的人越來越少，且新多益又走國際風，因此使用的名字可能不只我們常在考試中聽到的John、Susan，還會有一些來自世界各國的名字，如這題的蘇利亞。聽到這些不習慣的名字，我們直覺可能會把它當作一個生字而心臟漏跳一拍，但這一題並不要求你瞭解這個名字，只要能從對話中判斷這個人與兩人是同事就好了。其中(B)選項的「work for」是「替……工作」的意思，雖然乍看之下好像也可以選，但由蘇利亞敢叫男子與女子替她做事推斷，她不太可能是男子與女子的下屬，所以不選(B)。

2. 男子要女子做什麼？

(A) **撐箱子。**

(B) 把海報拿下來。

(C) 招呼客戶。

(D) 請蘇利亞去別的地方。

對話中，男子請女子撐箱子與搬文件，並沒有請女子拿下海報，拿海報的事是女子自己提出的。另外兩個選項也都不是女子要做的事，因此選**(A)**。

3. 男子與女子為什麼在清掃？

(A) 因為他們的朋友要到他們家來。

(B) 因為蘇利亞要到他們的套房來。

(C) 因為蘇利亞要他們的海報。

(D) **因為有些客戶要過來。**

抓準一段對話的內容，一開始的第一個步驟就是要立刻確認這個對話所發生的場景。我們一開始由「辦公室」與「客戶」這些詞語，很快能判斷這是在工作場所進行的對話，因此馬上能剔除前三個選項，選(D)。

多益聽力搶分有祕密，全真模擬試題13

1. What does the man most likely do?　　　　🎧 **Track 13**

   (A) He is most likely an office worker.

   (B) He is most likely a doctor.

   (C) He most likely delivers things.

   (D) He is most likely a cook.

2. Who is Mr. Park?

   (A) He is probably the woman's friend.

   (B) He is probably the woman's brother.

   (C) He is probably the woman's coworker.

   (D) He is probably the woman's son.

3. What do we know about Mr. Park?

   (A) He ordered a chair.

   (B) He tells the woman about everything he does.

   (C) He sits by the window.

   (D) He is not in right now.

GO ON TO THE NEXT PAGE ➡

多益聽力搶分有祕密，
全真模擬試題-P063頁答案與詳解

題目解答

1. (C)　　　　　　2. (C)　　　　　　3. (D)

聽力原文

M: Excuse me, where do I put this desk?

W: Huh? We didn't order a desk. This office is cramped as it is.

M: You sure did! Good thing I have the order printed out to prove it. See?

W: Ah, I see, Mr. Park must have ordered it without telling us. Um, can you leave it there by the window? We'll figure out where to put it when the guy who ordered it returns.

> **搶分重點**　◆ 口音為英國（男）與美國（女）。

聽力中譯

M：不好意思，這桌子放哪裡？

W：啊？我們沒有訂桌子啊，這辦公室已經夠擠了。

M：你們有訂啊！還好我有印訂單證明。看到了沒？

W：喔，我瞭解了，朴先生一定是沒跟我們講就訂了。呃，你可以把它擺在窗戶旁邊那裡嗎？等訂了它的那個人回來，我們再決定把它放在哪裡。

聽力題目詳解

1. 男子很可能是做什麼的？

(A) 他很可能是上班族。

(B) 他很可能是醫生。

(C) 他很可能以運送貨物為職。

(D) 他很可能是廚師。

多益聽力搶分有祕密，滿分高手10秒解題關鍵

對話的一開始，我們聽到男子搬了桌子進來，後來我們又聽到他掏出訂貨單，可見他很可能是運送貨物的人。當然，他也可能是廠商的人，直接將桌子親自送來，但沒有這個選項，因此選(C)。

2. 朴先生是誰？

(A) 他很可能是女子的朋友。

(B) 他很可能是女子的兄弟。

(C) 他很可能是女子的同事。

(D) 他很可能是女子的兒子。

多益聽力搶分有祕密，滿分高手10秒解題關鍵

由女子的自言自語中，聽到「辦公室已經很擠了」，可知對話進行的場景是辦公室。而女子又用了Mr.這個稱呼，可見她和朴先生不太可能是親戚或比較熟的朋友，因此選(C)最為可能。

3. 有關朴先生，我們知道什麼訊息？

(A) 他訂了一張椅子。

(B) 他做什麼都會告訴女子。

(C) 他坐在窗邊。

(D) 他現在不在。

多益聽力搶分有祕密，滿分高手10秒解題關鍵

朴先生訂了一張桌子，如果他現在在現場，理應告訴女子桌子是他訂的，而不是讓她在那邊跟送貨人員否認有訂桌子。再加上女子最後説「等他回來後」（when the guy who ordered it returns），可見朴先生現在不在。

多益聽力搶分有祕密，全真模擬試題14

1. What does the man most likely do?   🎧 **Track 14**

   (A) He is most likely a truck driver.

   (B) He is most likely a taxi driver.

   (C) He is most likely a police officer.

   (D) He most likely works in a hotel.

2. Why does the woman want the man to hurry?

   (A) She lost her contact lenses.

   (B) She needs to make a call.

   (C) She needs to meet her clients very soon.

   (D) Her flight is about to take off.

3. What do we know about the woman?

   (A) She lost her phone.

   (B) She doesn't have a way to contact her clients.

   (C) She is heading to her clients' house.

   (D) She needs to meet her clients in 10 minutes.

GO ON TO THE NEXT PAGE ➡

多益聽力搶分有祕密，全真模擬試題-P067頁答案與詳解

題目解答

1. **(B)**　　　　2. **(C)**　　　　3. **(D)**

聽力原文

W: How long does it take to get to the Plaza Hotel?

M: Around half an hour, if the traffic is fine.

W: Oh, no... I'm supposed to meet my clients in 10 minutes! Can you hurry?

M: I'll try, but no guarantees. You should call your clients first^英 and make some excuses, such as "I lost my contact lenses" or something.

W: Great, thanks for the suggestion! I'll call them up.

> **搶分重點**
> ❶ 口音為英國（男）與美國（女）。
> ❷ 在英國腔中，有些字的「r」音不會像美國腔中有明顯的捲舌。聽聽看男子怎麼發「first」的吧！

聽力中譯

W：到廣場飯店要多久？

M：大概半個小時，如果交通順暢的話。

W：噢不，我得在十分鐘內見客戶耶，你可以開快一點嗎？

M：我會盡量，不過不能保證。妳可以先打給客戶，掰個藉口，像是「我隱形眼鏡掉了」之類的。

W：好耶，感謝你的建議！我來打給他們。

聽力題目詳解

1. 男子很可能是做什麼的？

    (A) 他很可能是卡車司機。

    (B) 他很可能是計程車司機。

    (C) 他很可能是警察。

    (D) 他很可能在旅館上班。

多益聽力搶分有祕密，滿分高手**10秒解題關鍵**

雖然女子急著要趕去旅館，但不代表男子在那裡上班。從女子催男子開快一點看來，他很可能是計程車司機，畢竟要求卡車司機載妳到旅館見客戶實在太強人所難了。因此雖然整段對話都沒有提到「計程車」，我們依然能推理出(B)為正確答案。

---

2. 女子為何要男子快點？

    (A) 她的隱形眼鏡掉了。

    (B) 她必須打電話。

    (C) 她很快就要見客戶了。

    (D) 她要搭的飛機要飛了。

3. 關於女子，我們知道哪些事？

　　(A) 她把手機弄丟了。

　　(B) 她沒有辦法聯絡客戶。

　　(C) 她要前往客戶的家。

　　(D) 她在10分鐘內要見她的客戶。

多益聽力搶分有祕密，全真模擬試題15

1. Why is the man in a hurry to get down to work?　🎧 **Track 15**

    (A) He has a meeting to go to soon.

    (B) He has to read the woman's proposal.

    (C) He has to take the woman out to dinner.

    (D) He has to run into the meeting room.

2. How does the man feel towards the woman?

    (A) He feels sad about her.

    (B) He feels angry at her.

    (C) He feels grateful towards her.

    (D) He feels sick of her.

3. What does the man offer to do for the woman?

    (A) To edit her proposal.

    (B) To treat her to dinner.

    (C) To take her to the meeting.

    (D) To meet her clients for her.

GO ON TO THE NEXT PAGE

題目解答

1. (A)　　　　2. (C)　　　　3. (B)

聽力原文

W: I see several flaws in your proposal. I listed them out for you so that you can edit the whole thing before you meet the clients.

M: Thanks! I knew asking you to proofread before I go charging into the meeting room was a good idea.

W: No problem. But you have to hurry with those corrections though; your meeting starts in two hours.

M: I know! I'll get down to work now, and maybe treat you to dinner as a token of thanks!

> **搶分重點**　🔊 口音為英國（男）與美國（女）。

聽力中譯

W： 你的提案裡有好幾個缺失，我幫你列出來了，你見客戶前就可以再整個修正一下。

M： 謝啦！我就知道進會議室前找妳幫我校訂是對的。

W： 沒問題，不過你得改快一點，你兩小時內就要開會了。

M： 我知道啊！我現在就開始工作。為了感謝妳，晚上可能會請妳吃晚餐！

聽力題目詳解

1. 為什麼男子急著要開始工作？

   (A) 他很快要去開會了。

   (B) 他得讀女子的提案。

   (C) 他得帶女子去吃晚餐。

   (D) 他得跑進會議室。

多益聽力搶分有祕密，滿分高手10秒解題關鍵

由整個對話可得知，男子要在會議上提案，而會議兩個小時後要開始，但他的提案卻還有一部分需要修改，因此他才急著要工作，因此選(A)。

2. 男子對女子有什麼感覺？

   (A) 他為她的事感到傷心。

   (B) 他對她生氣。

   (C) 他很感激她。

   (D) 他受不了她。

多益聽力搶分有祕密，滿分高手10秒解題關鍵

男子對女子可能有各種不同的感覺，只是他沒在對話中讓我們知道。但聽力測驗的時間又短又緊湊，我們沒有時間天馬行空地想像男子與女子的關係，所以只能用對話中的內容，判斷男子應該很感激女子幫他校訂提案，選擇(C)。

3. 男子主動說要替女子做什麼？

(A) 替她修訂提案。

(B) 請她吃晚餐。

(C) 帶她去開會。

(D) 替她見客戶。

多益聽力搶分有祕密，滿分高手10秒解題關鍵

男子在最後一句中說到為了感謝女子而要請她吃晚餐，所以我們知道要選(B)。如果漏聽了這句，也應該能利用刪去法將(C)與(D)刪去，因為這些事情在工作上似乎不是男子可以擅自決定的，而且被硬帶去開會、客戶被搶走，似乎也不會讓女子感到開心。

多益聽力搶分有祕密，全真模擬試題16

1. Why does the woman need to go to Shanghai?　🎧 **Track 16**

   (A) She has to take a train.

   (B) She is going tomorrow.

   (C) She has a date there.

   (D) She is going to drive.

2. Who might the man most likely be?

   (A) He might be the woman's grandfather.

   (B) He might be the woman's boss.

   (C) He might be the woman's employee.

   (D) He might be the woman's doctor.

3. Why does the woman have to cancel her date?

   (A) There's no way she can get there in time.

   (B) Steve lost her ticket.

   (C) She does not like trains.

   (D) She didn't want to clean up the mess.

GO ON TO THE NEXT PAGE ➤

多益聽力搶分有祕密，
全真模擬試題-P075頁答案與詳解

題目解答

1. (C)   2. (C)   3. (A)

聽力原文

W: Steve, can you get me a train ticket to Shanghai[2] for tomorrow?

M: Wait, let me check... uh, all the trains to Shanghai tomorrow are booked.

W: Wow, I'll have to drive over then. Steve, look up online for me how long it will take for me to drive to this address.

M: Let me see. Oh, it takes about 26 hours.

W: What a mess! I guess I'll have to cancel the date then.

> **搶分重點**
>
> [1] 口音為英國（男）與美國（女）。
> [2] 在多益聽力測驗中，常會國際化地出現世界各地的地名。但我們知道，英語母語人士不可能全世界的地名都會唸，所以有時在對話中雖然聽到認識的地名，也會因為對方的念法和你習慣的不同而聽不懂。在這裡就算認不出「上海」兩字也不要慌張，從上文「a train ticket to...」應該可以判斷出這個生字是一個「地點」。

聽力中譯

W： 史帝夫，你可以幫我弄一張明天到上海的火車票嗎？

M： 等等喔，我看一下……啊，所有明天要去上海的火車都滿了。

W：哇，那我只好開車去了。史帝夫，幫我上網看一下我開車到
　　這個地址要多久。

M：我看看喔。喔，要花26個小時左右。

W：真是一團糟！我看我只能取消約會了。

聽力題目詳解

1. 女子為何要去上海？

　　(A) 她必須坐火車。

　　(B) 她明天要去。

　　(C) 她在那裡有約。

　　(D) 她要開車。

多益聽力搶分有祕密，滿分高手10秒解題關鍵

這題的關鍵就是搞懂題目問的是「時間」、「地點」、「如何」、
還是「為何」？只要知道這題想知道的是女子去上海的「原因」，
就能很快挑出答案了。

---

2. 男子最可能是誰？

　　(A) 他可能是女子的爺爺。

　　(B) 他可能是女子的老闆。

　　(C) 他可能是女子的屬下。

　　(D) 他可能是女子的醫師。

這題有一定的難度，因為整段對話中並未清楚說明兩人之間的關係。然而，我們可以從對話的口氣判斷男子與女子「不可能」是什麼關係。由女子直呼男子名諱，而且還到處使喚他，可見男子不太可能是女子的長輩或頂頭上司。一般而言，我們也不會叫自己的醫師替自己查一些有的沒的，所以我們可以判斷在這四個選項中，男子「最」有可能是(C)。

---

3. 女子為什麼必須取消約會？

   (A) 她不可能及時趕到。

   (B) 史帝夫把她的票弄丟了。

   (C) 她不喜歡火車。

   (D) 她不想清理混亂。

雖然對話中指出，女子如果拚命地開26個小時的車，的確可以到達上海，但想必女子不會想要這麼做，因此選(A)，不可能及時趕到。

多益聽力搶分有祕密，全真模擬試題17

1. What do the man and woman do?　　　　　🎧 **Track 17**

   (A) They are politicians.

   (B) They work in an engineering company.

   (C) They major in performance arts.

   (D) They work in a school.

2. What are the man and woman discussing?

   (A) A new colleague.

   (B) Best schools to study in.

   (C) Performance arts.

   (D) Their company name.

3. What do we know about the new guy?

   (A) He studied performance arts.

   (B) He seems pretty smart.

   (C) He graduated from the woman's school.

   (D) He never talked to the man before.

GO ON TO THE NEXT PAGE

多益聽力搶分有祕密，
全真模擬試題-P079頁答案與詳解

題目解答

1. (B)　　　　2. (A)　　　　3. (B)

聽力原文

W: The new guy, Rasheed, seems pretty smart. Do you know where he graduated from?

M: Can't remember the name of the school, but I do know that he majored in political science.

W: What? A political science major in an engineering company? That's pretty unexpected!

M: I was surprised when he told me that too.

W: Look who's talking! Didn't you major in performance arts?

搶分重點　◀》口音為英國（男）與美國（女）。

聽力中譯

W：那個新來的叫拉西德的，感覺挺聰明的。你知道他哪裡畢業的嗎？

M：想不起來學校的名字了，但我知道他以前是主修政治的。

W：啊？主修政治，卻在工程公司工作？真沒想到！

M：他告訴我的時候，我也很驚訝。

W：輪不到你說吧，你不是主修表演藝術嗎？

聽力題目詳解

1. 男子與女子是做什麼的？

(A) 他們是政治家。

(B) 他們在工程公司工作。

(C) 他們主修表演藝術。

(D) 他們在學校工作。

多益聽力搶分有祕密，滿分高手10秒解題關鍵

兩人在對話中討論了不少科系相關的話題，不過到頭來他們還是
在女子所說的「engineering company」，工程公司中工作，要選
(B)。

2. 男子與女子在討論什麼？

(A) 新同事。

(B) 最好的學校。

(C) 表演藝術。

(D) 他們公司的名字。

多益聽力搶分有祕密，滿分高手10秒解題關鍵

男子與女子其實聊了不少話題，但其中並沒有涵蓋到念哪間學校最
好、公司的名字、或表演藝術的細節，可知還是選「新同事」最為
恰當。

3. 有關新來的那個男生,我們知道什麼事?

(A) 他唸過表演藝術。

(B) 他似乎很聰明。

(C) 他和女子同一所學校畢業。

(D) 他不曾和男子說過話。

多益聽力搶分有祕密,滿分高手10秒解題關鍵

我們知道念表演藝術的是說話的男子,而非新來的拉西德;我們不曉得新來的拉西德念的是什麼學校;但拉西德曾和對話中的男子提過自己念的科系,可知兩人曾經說過話,因此只能選擇(B)了。

多益聽力搶分有祕密，全真模擬試題18

1. Who is Mr. Wolinski most likely to be?　　　🎧 **Track 18**

   (A) He is likely the man and woman's nephew.

   (B) He is likely the man and woman's son.

   (C) He is likely the man and woman's boss.

   (D) He is likely the man and woman's student.

2. What is wrong with the woman?

   (A) She has a headache.

   (B) She has a fever.

   (C) She is dizzy.

   (D) She has a cough.

3. Why does the woman not want to take the afternoon off?

   (A) She is afraid of Mr. Wolinski.

   (B) She has a lot of work to do.

   (C) She expects to have a headache.

   (D) She doesn't want to see a doctor.

GO ON TO THE NEXT PAGE

多益聽力搶分有祕密，
全真模擬試題-P083頁答案與詳解

題目解答

1. (C)　　　　2. (A)　　　　3. (B)

聽力原文

W: I've got a headache. I think I'm coming down with a cold.

M: Eh? Do you want to ask for the afternoon off and go see a doctor^英? I'm sure Mr. Wolinski won't mind.

W: I still have a lot of work to do though. This project is due next week!

M: How do you expect to get work done with a headache? I suggest that you go home and rest a bit at least!

> **搶分重點**　❶ 口音為英國（男）與美國（女）。
> ❷ 英國腔的「doctor」發音和美國腔不同，不習慣的人可以多聽幾次這個字。

聽力中譯

W： 我頭痛，我想我要感冒了。

M： 是喔？你要不要請下午的假，去看個醫生？沃林斯基先生一定不會介意。

W： 可是我還有很多工作要做。這個案子下個禮拜就要交了！

M： 妳頭痛怎麼還做得了工作呢？我建議妳至少還是回家休息一下吧！

聽力題目詳解

1. 沃林斯基先生很可能是？

(A) 他可能是男子與女子的姪子。

(B) 他可能是男子與女子的兒子。

(C) 他可能是男子與女子的老闆。

(D) 他可能是男子與女子的學生。

多益聽力搶分有祕密，滿分高手**10秒**解題關鍵

在四個選項中，你或許可以發現有三個有共通點：姪子、兒子和學生都是在身分上處於比較下位的角色，只有「老闆」這個選項是居上位。而我們從男子稱沃林斯基先生為「先生」，與兩人提到女子要請假可能需要他同意這點，可判斷沃林斯基先生的地位應該是比兩人高的，因此可以立馬刪掉三個選項，而選擇「老闆」。有時在考試時先掃一遍答案，找到和別人不一樣的那一個，說不定就是正確的解答了喔！

2. 女子有什麼問題？

(A) 她頭痛。

(B) 她發燒。

(C) 她頭暈。

(D) 她咳嗽。

雖然發燒、頭暈、咳嗽的確都是感冒會有的症狀，但女子並沒有提到她有這些徵兆，只說她頭痛而已，因此選(A)。我們腦中常會把頭痛、發燒、頭暈等等資訊歸類在一起，混做一團來記憶，但在考聽力測驗這種有可能問得很精確的考試時，則不能記個大概就好，要記清楚。

3. 女子為何不想請下午的假？

　(A) 她害怕沃林斯基先生。

　(B) 她有很多工作要做。

　(C) 她預期會頭痛。

　(D) 她不想看醫生。

根據女子自己所說，她的工作很多，下個禮拜還有案子要交，所以她不想請假，並沒有提到其他的理由，所以選(B)。

多益聽力搶分有祕密，全真模擬試題19

1. Why does Andrew look mad?　　　　🎧 **Track 19**

   (A) He is angry at his clients.

   (B) He has a toothache.

   (C) He is angry at the woman.

   (D) He is angry at the man.

2. What does the woman think Andrew should do?

   (A) Pay everyone a million bucks.

   (B) See a dentist after work.

   (C) See a dentist now.

   (D) Stride around the place.

3. Which of these statements is NOT correct about Andrew?

   (A) He has a toothache.

   (B) He looks mad today.

   (C) He scared his clients away.

   (D) He wants to see a dentist after work.

GO ON TO THE NEXT PAGE ➡

多益聽力搶分有祕密，
全真模擬試題-P087頁答案與詳解

題目解答

1. (B)　　　　2. (C)　　　　3. (C)

聽力原文

W: Why does Andrew look so mad today? If he meets his clients with that face he's gonna scare them away.

M: Oh, it's because he's got a toothache. He's going[英] to see a dentist after work, I think.

W: Well, I think he should go see that dentist now! I don't want him striding around the place looking like everyone owed him a million bucks.

M: If you insist, I can talk to him I guess.

> **搶分重點**
> ① 口音為英國（男）與美國（女）。
> ② 聽聽看男子所説的，英國腔的「going」中，「go」和「ing」之間沒有明顯分成兩個音節，幾乎融成了一個音節。

聽力中譯

W：安德魯今天看起來怎麼這麼生氣？如果他用那張臉去見客戶，他們都會被嚇跑。

M：喔，那是因為他牙痛。他下班會去看牙醫的樣子。

W：我可是覺得他現在就該去看牙醫！我不要他帶著那張好像每個人都欠他一百萬的臉到處走。

M：妳堅持的話，我是可以跟他談談看啦。

聽力題目詳解

1. 安德魯為什麼看起來很生氣？

    (A) 他在生他客戶的氣。

    (B) 他牙痛。

    (C) 他在生女子的氣。

    (D) 他在生男子的氣。

多益聽力搶分有祕密，滿分高手10秒解題關鍵

由對話中我們可以判斷安德魯並沒有真的生氣，只是「看起來在生氣」而已，便可把所有與「生別人的氣」相關的選項都刪除，選出 (B)「他牙痛」。

---

2. 女子認為安德魯該做什麼？

    (A) 付每個人一百萬。

    (B) 下班去看牙醫。

    (C) 現在就去看牙醫。

    (D) 到處走。

多益聽力搶分有祕密，滿分高手10秒解題關鍵

雖然安德魯自己是想要下班後再去看牙醫，但女子認為他這張臭臉會嚇到人，所以認為他應該馬上去看牙醫，而不是等到下班，因此選(C)。

3. 下列哪個與安德魯有關的選項並非為真？

(A) 他牙痛。

(B) 他今天看起來很生氣。

(C) 他把客戶嚇走了。

(D) 他下班後要看牙醫。

多益聽力搶分有祕密，滿分高手10秒解題關鍵

女子自己想像著「安德魯接下來說不定會擺著臭臉去見客戶，把客戶都嚇跑」這個情境，但這都是她自己個人的想像，安德魯並沒有真的把客戶嚇跑，所以(C)選項並非為真，要選(C)。

多益聽力搶分有祕密，全真模擬試題20

1. Why does the woman want the man to come to the gym
   with her? 🎧 **Track 20**
   (A) She doesn't want to go by herself.
   (B) She thinks he is interested in yoga.
   (C) She thinks he should lose some weight.
   (D) She wants 10,000 a month.

2. Why does the man not want to go to the gym?
   (A) He would rather spend his money on food.
   (B) He would rather do aerobics.
   (C) He didn't like the woman.
   (D) He didn't like yoga.

3. What can you NOT do in the gym the woman goes to?
   (A) Take yoga classes.
   (B) Take aerobics classes.
   (C) Take cooking classes.
   (D) Use sports equipment.

GO ON TO THE NEXT PAGE ➤

多益聽力搶分有祕密，
全真模擬試題-P091頁答案與詳解

題目解答

1. (C)   2. (A)   3. (C)

....

聽力原文

W: You sure look round these days. You should come to the gym with me after work.

M: The gym? Nah, sounds super expensive.

W: It's actually quite cheap! You get to use all kinds of sports equipment, and take classes like yoga and aerobics. All for 10,000 dollars a month!

M: 10,000 a month? I'd rather^英 spend my money on food.

> **搶分重點**
> ❶ 口音為英國（男）與美國（女）。
> ❷ 英國腔的「rather」，特別是「ra」的音節，和美國腔不太一樣。

聽力中譯

W：你最近看起來真是圓滾滾。你下班應該跟我去健身房才對。

M：健身房？不要啦，聽起來超貴的。

W：其實很便宜啊！你可以用各式各樣的運動器材，還能上瑜伽與有氧運動的課程。一個月只要一萬呢！

M：一個月一萬？我還寧可把我的錢拿去買東西吃。

聽力題目詳解

1. 女子為什麼要男子和她一起去健身房？

   (A) 她不想自己去。

   (B) 她認為他對瑜伽有興趣。

   (C) 她認為他該減個幾公斤。

   (D) 她想要一個月一萬。

多益聽力搶分有祕密，滿分高手10秒解題關鍵

女子一開口就說男子看起來圓滾滾（真是傷感情），可見她認為他
應該減個幾公斤，所以要和她一起去健身房，因此選(C)。

2. 男子為什麼不想去健身房？

   (A) 他寧可把錢花在吃上。

   (B) 他寧可做有氧運動。

   (C) 他不喜歡女子。

   (D) 他不喜歡瑜伽。

多益聽力搶分有祕密，滿分高手10秒解題關鍵

男子在對話中並沒有提到自己喜歡或不喜歡什麼，但他卻說健身房
很貴，他寧願把錢拿去買吃的，可知要選(A)。

3. 在女子去的健身房，你無法做什麼？

(A) 上瑜伽課。

(B) 上有氧運動課。

(C) 上烹飪課。

(D) 使用運動器材。

多益聽力搶分有祕密，滿分高手10秒解題關鍵

在女子開始列舉健身房的種種好處時，仔細聽，會發現女子提到了瑜伽、有氧課程與運動器材。就算不小心漏聽了，也可以依常理判斷女子常去的健身房沒有提供烹飪課程，所以選擇(C)。

多益聽力搶分有祕密，全真模擬試題21

1. Why is the man exhausted?　　　　🎧 **Track 21**

   (A) Because he has to run marathons.

   (B) Because he has to talk to his boss.

   (C) Because he injured his toe.

   (D) Because he does not want to see the woman.

2. What is true about the man?

   (A) He likes running marathons.

   (B) He is injured.

   (C) He often disobeys his boss.

   (D) He looks exhausted these days.

3. What do we know about the man's boss?

   (A) Something is wrong with his toe.

   (B) He likes running marathons.

   (C) He invited the man to his house.

   (D) He is always exhausted.

GO ON TO THE NEXT PAGE

題目解答

1. **(A)**　　　2. **(D)**　　　3. **(B)**

聽力原文

W: Hey, are you doing okay? You always look so exhausted these days.

M: I know. It's just that my boss recently got into running marathons these days, and he "invited" us to run with him. Who could say no?

W: Aw, you're not a marathon person, are you? How about you tell him you injured your toe and can't run?

M: Good idea! I'll do just that.

搶分重點 🔊 口音為英國（男）與美國（女）。

聽力中譯

W：喂，你還好嗎？你最近看起來都超累的。

M：我知道啊，只是我老闆最近忽然迷上跑馬拉松，而且還「邀請」我們跟他一起跑。誰敢說不要啊？

W：唉，你不愛跑馬拉松，對不對？跟他說你腳趾受傷，不能跑步怎麼樣？

M：好主意！我就這麼做吧。

聽力題目詳解

1. 男子為什麼這麼累？

   (A) 因為他必須跑馬拉松。

   (B) 因為他必須和老闆交談。

   (C) 因為他傷到了腳趾。

   (D) 因為他不想見那個女子。

多益聽力搶分有祕密，滿分高手10秒解題關鍵

男子疲累的原因雖然和老闆相關，但並非與老闆交談讓他很累，而是老闆要求他跑馬拉松讓他很累，所以選(A)。傷到腳趾的事是女子捏造的，男子並非真的有傷到腳趾。

---

2. 有關男子，何者為真？

   (A) 他喜歡跑馬拉松。

   (B) 他受傷了。

   (C) 他常不聽老闆的話。

   (D) 他最近看起來很累。

多益聽力搶分有祕密，滿分高手10秒解題關鍵

女子一開始就說男子最近看起來很累，也就是這題的答案(D)。至於其他的選項，男子不喜歡跑馬拉松、也並沒有受傷。從他不敢拒絕老闆的馬拉松邀請可知，如果連這件事都不敢拒絕，其他事他恐怕也不敢拒絕，所以他應該不會經常不聽老闆的話，不可選(C)。

3. 關於男子的老闆，我們知道什麼事？

(A) 他的腳趾有點問題。

(B) 他喜歡跑馬拉松。

(C) 他邀請男子到他家。

(D) 他總是很累。

多益聽力搶分有祕密，滿分高手10秒解題關鍵

在這個簡短的對話中，真正提到男子老闆的內容不多，我們只知道老闆喜歡跑馬拉松，還喜歡拉員工一起跑。因此，我們就可以選出(B)這個答案，因為其他的選項在對話中完全和老闆無關。

多益聽力搶分有祕密，全真模擬試題22

1. Who is Mr. Jacobson most likely to be?　　　🎧 **Track 22**

   (A) He is likely the man's colleague.

   (B) He likely works in the woman's company.

   (C) He is likely the woman's friend.

   (D) He is likely the man's driver.

2. What do we know about the man?

   (A) He has an appointment at 11 o'clock.

   (B) He has lost his way.

   (C) He is driving a car.

   (D) He wants to visit landmarks.

3. What do we know about the woman?

   (A) She works at Stardance Studios.

   (B) She has lost her way.

   (C) She has an appointment with Mr. Jacobson.

   (D) She doesn't know where she is.

GO ON TO THE NEXT PAGE

多益聽力搶分有祕密，
全真模擬試題-P099頁答案與詳解

題目解答

1. (B)　　　　2. (B)　　　　3. (A)

....

聽力原文

W: Hello, this is Stardance Studios. What can we do for you?

M: May I have the directions② to your building? I've got an appointment with Mr. Jacobson at 10 o'clock, but I'm afraid I've lost my way.

W: I see. Please tell me where you are right now and I'll point out some landmarks for you.

M: The problem is I don't even know where I am!

W: In that case, I suggest that you use the GPS system on your phone.

> **搶分重點**
> ❶ 口音為英國（男）與美國（女）。
> ❷ 「directions」這個字的第一個音節，有些人會唸成「底」的音，然而也有些人會唸「ㄞ」，如這裡的男子就是。這要看個人的習慣，和國家不一定完全相關。

聽力中譯

W： 您好，這裡是星舞工作坊。我們可以如何幫助您呢？

M： 可以告訴我怎麼去你們大樓嗎？我和約考伯森先生十點有約，但我恐怕迷路了。

W： 我瞭解了。請告訴我您現在在哪裡，我會指出一些地標給您。

M：問題是我連我自己在哪都不知道了！

W：那樣的話，我建議您使用手機上的GPS系統。

聽力題目詳解

1. 約考伯森先生最可能是誰？

(A) 他可能是男子的同事。

(B) 他可能在女子的公司工作。

(C) 他可能是女子的朋友。

(D) 他可能是男子的司機。

多益聽力搶分有祕密，滿分高手10秒解題關鍵

由男子打電話到女的公司，和她説要去找約考伯森先生這一點可得
知：約考伯森先生應該是和女子在同一個地方工作。當然，他也可
能是女子的朋友，但對話裡面並沒有提到兩人之間的感情糾葛，所
以我們選擇(B)。

2. 關於男子，我們知道什麼事？

(A) 他在十一點的時候有約。

(B) 他迷路了。

(C) 他在開車。

(D) 他想拜訪地標。

在聽完一個對話時，可以試試快速歸納出這段對話的主旨。以上這段對話的主旨就是「男子迷路了」，因此可以迅速選出(B)的答案。

3. 關於女子，我們知道什麼事？

    (A) **她在星舞工作坊工作。**

    (B) 她迷路了。

    (C) 她和約考伯森先生有約。

    (D) 她不知道自己在哪裡。

除了(A)是女子的情形以外，其他三個選項都是在講男子，只要搞清楚題目問的是男子還是女子，就能回答這個問題。

多益聽力搶分有祕密，全真模擬試題23

1. What do we know about Mr. Braun?　　　🎧 **Track 23**

　　(A) He is in the Public Relations Department.

　　(B) He does not know the woman.

　　(C) He is not in his office now.

　　(D) He does not work in the same company as the man.

2. What do we know about the woman?

　　(A) She works at the Institute of Technology.

　　(B) She is good friends with the man.

　　(C) She does not want to leave a message on the phone.

　　(D) Her job is to transfer calls.

3. What is true about the man?

　　(A) He works in the Public Relations Department.

　　(B) He does not want to help transfer calls.

　　(C) He is on good terms with Mr. Braun.

　　(D) Picking up phone calls is a part of his job.

GO ON TO THE NEXT PAGE

多益聽力搶分有祕密，
全真模擬試題-P103頁答案與詳解

題目解答

1. **(A)**　　　2. **(A)**　　　3. **(D)**

聽力原文

W: Hello. I would like to speak to Mr. Braun in the Public Relations Department, please.

M: I see. Please hold on and I'll transfer^英 your call.

W: Thank you.

M: I'm sorry, but that number is currently engaged. Would you like to leave a message?

W: Sure. Please let him know that Tanya from the Institute of Technology called to confirm the appointment next Wednesday.

> **搶分重點**
> ❶ 口音為英國（男）與美國（女）。
> ❷ 英國腔中常習慣字尾的r不捲舌發音，這裡的「transfer」就是一個例子。

聽力中譯

W：您好，我想找公關部的布朗先生。

M：我瞭解了，請不要掛斷，我替您轉接。

W：謝謝。

M：抱歉，他的號碼現在在通話中，您想留言嗎？

W：好啊，請讓他知道科技機構的潭雅打來確認下禮拜三的約會。

聽力題目詳解

1. 有關布朗先生，我們知道什麼事？

   (A) 他在公關部門工作。

   (B) 他不認識女子。

   (C) 他現在不在辦公室。

   (D) 他和男子不在同一個公司工作。

多益聽力搶分有祕密，滿分高手10秒解題關鍵

這題有個模稜兩可的陷阱(C)。依對話內容判斷，布朗先生的電話在通話中，可知他人在辦公室，且正在通電話，所以(C)的內容不為真。但也會有人認為可能是他電話沒掛好，或有別人使用他的電話，並不能因此判斷他不在辦公室。不過，這題並非要你判斷布朗先生在不在辦公室，而是要你選出「確定為真」的選項，因此，回答問題時不必花太多時間鑽研「可能為真、也可能不為真」的選項，而選「100%一定是真的」的選項即可。

---

2. 關於女子，我們知道什麼事？

   (A) 她在科技機構工作。

   (B) 她和男子是好友。

   (C) 她不想電話留言。

   (D) 她的工作是轉接電話。

女子在留言時，說她是科技機構的潭雅，可知她應該是在科技機構工作，所以選(A)。至於她和男子的關係、工作是什麼，對話中並沒有提到。

---

3. 關於男子，何者為真？

　(A) 他在公關部工作。

　(B) 他不想幫忙轉接電話。

　(C) 他和布朗先生是好友。

　(D) 接電話是他工作的一部分。

男子替女子將電話轉接至公關部，可知他人並不在公關部，也不介意幫忙轉接電話，所以(A)和(B)都是不適合選的選項。男子的工作雖然不見得只有接電話這一項，但從他很自然地接起電話、完全沒有不高興或困惑聽起來，接電話對他來說應該是習以為常的事，所以「(D)接電話是他工作的一部分」應該是正確的。

多益聽力搶分有祕密，全真模擬試題24

1. Where does the man most likely work?　　🎧 **Track 24**

   (A) On the subway.

   (B) In a restaurant.

   (C) At the dentist's.

   (D) In the evening.

2. Where is the woman?

   (A) She is at the dentist's.

   (B) She is on the subway.

   (C) She is making an appointment.

   (D) She is going to the dentist's.

3. Why can't the woman hear the man?

   (A) The connection is bad.

   (B) Her phone is out of battery.

   (C) He is speaking too softly.

   (D) It is too noisy.

GO ON TO THE NEXT PAGE

多益聽力搶分有祕密，
全真模擬試題-P107頁答案與詳解

題目解答

1. **(C)**   2. **(B)**   3. **(D)**

聽力原文

M: Hello, Mrs. Wattenberg. I'm calling to remind you that you have a dentist's appointment with us tomorrow, at 7 in the evening.

W: Huh? Sorry, can you repeat that?

M: You've got a dentist's appointment with us tomorrow at 7. ❷

W: Pardon? Ugh, sorry, it's a bit hard to hear you. I'm on the subway and it's kind of noisy.

M: I see. I'll call you back later.

> **搶分重點**
> ❶ 口音為英國（男）與美國（女）。
> ❷ 這句男子念得較慢，並一個字一個字分開來強調。這是因為女子似乎聽不懂他講話，所以他為了讓她聽清楚，而特別選擇慢慢說。

聽力中譯

M： 您好，瓦騰堡小姐。我打來是要通知妳，妳明天晚上七點有預約要來我們這裡看牙醫。

W： 啊？不好意思，你可以再說一次嗎？

M： 妳明天七點有預約要來我們這裡看牙醫。

W： 你說什麼？唉，抱歉。有點難聽到你講話。我在地鐵上，有點吵。

M： 我瞭解了。我待會再打給您。

聽力題目詳解

1. 男子很可能在哪裡工作？

　　(A) 在地鐵。

　　(B) 在餐廳。

　　(C) 在牙醫診所。

　　(D) 在晚上。

多益聽力搶分有祕密，滿分高手**10秒**解題關鍵

男子打電話通知女子要去看牙醫，而且還說「跟我們有預約」，從「我們」可知男子應該是牙醫診所的工作人員，所以選(C)。

2. 女子在哪裡？

　　(A) 她在牙醫診所。

　　(B) 她在地鐵上。

　　(C) 她在預約。

　　(D) 她正要去看牙醫。

多益聽力搶分有祕密，滿分高手**10秒**解題關鍵

對話中，女子說自己在地鐵上，當然也有可能是在說謊，但由牙醫診所打來通知預約事宜可知女子一定不在牙醫診所，也不在去看牙醫的路上，所以我們只能選(B)。

3. 女子為什麼聽不到男子說話？

(A) 手機訊號很差。

(B) 她的手機沒電。

(C) 他講話太小聲了。

(D) 太吵了。

多益聽力搶分有祕密，滿分高手10秒解題關鍵

女子位於地鐵這種人多嘈雜且行駛聲音很大的地方，可想而知一定很吵，所以她聽不到男子講話。女子並未提及手機有問題，或叫男子講大聲一點，所以其他選項都不可選。

多益聽力搶分有祕密，全真模擬試題25

1. Who are the man and woman most likely to be? 🎧 **Track 25**

   (A) Mother and son.

   (B) Colleagues.

   (C) Twins.

   (D) Enemies.

2. Why can't the man go to the meeting?

   (A) He has to go to Hong Kong.

   (B) He is in Hong Kong now.

   (C) He is buying snacks.

   (D) He is going in the woman's place.

3. What do we know about the woman?

   (A) She is unwilling to help the man.

   (B) She doesn't like snacks.

   (C) She will be going to the meeting tomorrow.

   (D) She will fly to Hong Kong.

GO ON TO THE NEXT PAGE

多益聽力搶分有祕密，
全真模擬試題-P111頁答案與詳解

題目解答

1. (B)　　　　　2. (A)　　　　　3. (C)

聽力原文

M: I'm afraid I won't be able to make it to the meeting tomorrow. Can you go in my place?

W: Sure, but why won't you be able to make it? You've never been absent to a meeting before.

M: I have to fly to Hong Kong tonight because something urgent came up. It's kind of an emergency.

W: I see. Fine, I'll cover for you. But do bring me some Hong Kong snacks!

> **搶分重點** 🔈 口音為英國（男）與美國（女）。

聽力中譯

M： 我明天恐怕無法去開會，妳可以代替我去嗎？

W： 可以啊，可是你為什麼沒辦法去開會？你從來沒哪次開會缺席的。

M： 發生了急事，我今晚得飛去香港。狀況有點緊急。

W： 我瞭解了。好啊，我會幫你忙，不過要幫我帶香港點心回來喔！

聽力題目詳解

1. 男子與女子很可能是？

(A) 母子。

(B) 同事。

(C) 雙胞胎。

(D) 敵人。

多益聽力搶分有祕密，滿分高手10秒解題關鍵

只要想想四個選項中，哪個符合「男子請女子代替他去開會」的情境，這題就能迎刃而解。兒子一般不會叫媽媽替他去開會，敵人也不會；雖然雙胞胎可以偽裝成對方去開會，似乎很歡樂，但兩人也沒有提到自己是雙胞胎的事，可知還是選(B)最為合理。

---

2. 男子為何不能去開會？

(A) 他要去香港。

(B) 他人在香港。

(C) 他在買點心。

(D) 他要代替女子去。

多益聽力搶分有祕密，滿分高手10秒解題關鍵

男子說「晚上要飛去香港」，可知他人現在並沒有在香港，而是因為明天可能還在香港而無法參加明天的會議，所以選(A)。

3. 關於女子，我們知道什麼事？

(A) 她不願意幫助男子。

(B) 她不喜歡點心。

(C) 她明天要去開會。

(D) 她會飛去香港。

多益聽力搶分有祕密，滿分高手10秒解題關鍵

女子答應明天要代替男子去開會，既然是已經答應的事情，那她明天除非有什麼意外，不然應該一定會去開會的，可知要選(C)。

多益聽力搶分有祕密，全真模擬試題26

1. Where did this conversation likely happen?　🎧 **Track 26**

　　(A) At a meeting.

　　(B) At an interview.

　　(C) At a party.

　　(D) At a concert.

2. What do we know about the woman?

　　(A) She is a Harvard graduate.

　　(B) She graduated one year ago.

　　(C) She studied physics.

　　(D) She got a masters degree this year.

3. Why does the woman think she qualifies for the job?

　　(A) She is very kind-hearted.

　　(B) She has good people skills.

　　(C) She has related intern experience.

　　(D) She is very cheerful.

GO ON TO THE NEXT PAGE

多益聽力搶分有祕密，
全真模擬試題-P115頁答案與詳解

題目解答

1. (B)　　　　　2. (A)　　　　　3. (C)

聽力原文

M: Would you introduce yourself first?

W: Sure. I am a Harvard graduate in biochemistry. I got my bachelor's degree this year. Now I am looking for a job related to my major.

M: Why do you believe you are qualified for this job?

W: I have intern experience in this field and am an efficient[2] worker as well as an eager learner.

搶分重點

❶ 口音為英國（男）與美國（女）。

❷ 「and am an efficient」這幾個字都是由母音開始，而英文中習慣將母音開頭的字和前一個字結尾的子音連在一起念，因此在聽這段時幾乎找不到斷開的地方，要仔細聽清楚才能分出哪個字是哪個字。

聽力中譯

M： 請先自我介紹好嗎？

W： 好的。我是哈佛大學生物化學系的畢業生，我今年拿到了學士學位。我現在在找一個和主修科系相關的工作。

M： 為什麼妳認為妳適任這個工作呢？

W： 我在這個領域有實習經驗，而且是個有效率的工作者，也是個積極的學習者。

聽力題目詳解

1. 這個對話很可能是在哪裡發生的？

(A) 在會議中。

(B) 在面試中。

(C) 在派對中。

(D) 在演唱會中。

多益聽力搶分有祕密，滿分高手10秒解題關鍵

男子詢問女子為何覺得自己適任這個工作，可知女子應該是要找工作，而兩人對話的場景很可能就是「面試」。

---

2. 關於女子，我們知道什麼事？

(A) 她是哈佛的畢業生。

(B) 她是一年前畢業的。

(C) 她是念物理的。

(D) 她今年拿到碩士學位。

多益聽力搶分有祕密，滿分高手10秒解題關鍵

從女子的自我介紹中，我們聽到幾個大重點：她是哈佛畢業的、她念的是生物化學、她今年拿到學士學位。只要知道這幾個重點，就能很容易地選出(A)的答案。

3. 女子為什麼覺得自己適任這個工作？

(A) 她很善良。

(B) 她有良好的人際手腕。

(C) 她有相關的實習經驗。

(D) 她很開朗。

多益聽力搶分有祕密，全真模擬試題27

1. What does the man offer to do for the woman?　🎧 **Track 27**

   (A) To get a magazine for her.

   (B) To find Mrs. Johanssen for her.

   (C) To bring her tea.

   (D) To turn down the air conditioner.

2. What do we know about the woman?

   (A) She has an appointment at eleven.

   (B) She doesn't want tea.

   (C) She doesn't want to wait for Mrs. Johanssen.

   (D) She is not available at the moment.

3. What does the woman think about the man's office?

   (A) It offers cold tea.

   (B) It is too cold.

   (C) It doesn't have enough magazines.

   (D) It should be open soon.

GO ON TO THE NEXT PAGE

多益聽力搶分有祕密，
全真模擬試題-P119頁答案與詳解

題目解答

1. (C)   2. (A)   3. (B)

聽力原文

M: Good morning. May I help you?

W: Good morning. I have an appointment with Mrs. Johanssen at eleven.

M: Mrs. Johanssen? Ah, I'm afraid she is not available at the moment, but I expect that she will be back soon. Please wait here and grab a magazine. I'll get you some tea.

W: Great, thanks. Brr, don't you get cold in here? Your office sure is freezing!

> **搶分重點** 🔊 口音為英國（男）與美國（女）。

聽力中譯

M：早安，我能幫妳什麼嗎？

W：早安，我和喬涵森太太在十一點有約。

M：喬涵森太太？啊，她恐怕現在不在，不過我預期她很快會回來。請在這裡等著，拿本雜誌看。我幫您倒茶。

W：好啊，謝謝。唉呀，你不冷嗎？你們辦公室真的很冷啊！

聽力題目詳解

1. 男子自願要為女子做什麼？

    (A) 幫她拿雜誌。

    (B) 幫她找喬涵森太太。

    (C) 幫她拿茶來。

    (D) 把冷氣調小。

多益聽力搶分有祕密，滿分高手10秒解題關鍵

男子請女子自己拿一本雜誌，等喬涵森太太回來，可知答案不會是 (A)或(B)。雖然女子確實抗議說辦公室太冷了，但對話中男子並沒有說要去動冷氣，所以我們也無法單憑自己的延伸想像選擇(D)，畢竟男子說不定不願意或無法調冷氣呢。

2. 關於女子，我們知道什麼事？

    (A) 她十一點有約。

    (B) 她不想要茶。

    (C) 她不想等喬涵森太太。

    (D) 她現在不在。

多益聽力搶分有祕密，滿分高手10秒解題關鍵

女子與喬涵森太太十一點有約，可知(A)選項是正確的。本題沒有太多混淆視聽的時間選項，所以只要抓準「十一點」這個關鍵，就能正確回答。

3. 關於男子的辦公室，女子覺得如何？

(A) 有冷茶可以喝。

(B) 太冷了。

(C) 雜誌太少了。

(D) 快開了。

多益聽力搶分有祕密，滿分高手10秒解題關鍵

女子和男子抗議辦公室太冷，並未提到茶冷了、或雜誌不夠等問題，所以選(B)。

多益聽力搶分有祕密，全真模擬試題28

1. What is the notice about?　　　　　　　🎧 **Track 28**

    (A) A surprise baby shower.

    (B) A surprise birthday party.

    (C) A surprise dance-off.

    (D) A surprise concert.

2. What should the recipients of the notice do?

    (A) Gather at the 3rd floor, 4 p.m. Friday.

    (B) Bring lots of food.

    (C) Come to the office on Saturday.

    (D) Tell Susannah about the notice.

3. What will the woman do?

    (A) Type a letter to Susannah.

    (B) Type out a notice.

    (C) Finish a project.

    (D) Bring party hats.

GO ON TO THE NEXT PAGE

題目解答

1. (B)   2. (A)   3. (B)

聽力原文

M: Jenna, can you type up a notice for me and send it to everyone in our project group?

W: Certainly. What would you like to say on the notice?

M: Let me see... surprise birthday party for Susannah next Friday, 4 p.m. on the 3rd floor. Bring drinks. That's probably all.

W: Okay, I'll type that up.

M: Wait, remember not to send one to Susannah! It's a surprise!

搶分重點 🔊 口音為英國（男）與美國（女）。

聽力中譯

M： 珍娜，妳可以幫我打一張公告，寄給我們案子團隊的所有人嗎？

W： 當然可以。你想在公告上寫什麼？

M： 我想想看……蘇珊娜驚喜生日派對，下個星期五下午四點，在三樓，帶喝的來。大概就這樣。

W： 好，我會打出來。

M： 等等，記得不要寄給蘇珊娜，是驚喜喔！

聽力題目詳解

1. 公告的內容是什麼？

(A) 驚喜新生兒派對。

(B) 驚喜生日派對。

(C) 驚喜尬舞比賽。

(D) 驚喜演唱會。

多益聽力搶分有祕密，滿分高手10秒解題關鍵

男子和女子提到要為蘇珊娜辦一場生日派對，而這也是女子將打在公告中的內容。如果不小心漏聽了這項重要的資訊，也可以判斷一般不會在「星期五下午四點」這種尷尬的時間，在公司大樓裡舉辦演唱會或尬舞比賽，而可以刪除一些選項。

2. 接到公告的人該做什麼？

(A) 在星期五下午四點，在三樓集合。

(B) 帶很多食物。

(C) 在星期六到辦公室。

(D) 告訴蘇珊娜公告的事。

就算一下慌張沒有記下派對的確切地點與時間，也可以用刪去法判斷這題的答案。男子只請大家帶喝的，沒有叫大家帶很多食物，也沒有請大家在非上班日來公司，因此可以刪掉這兩項。至於(D)，雖然男子沒有明說不能告訴蘇珊娜公告的事，但所有接到公告的人應該都心知肚明，驚喜派對的事不能事先讓派對主角知道，可見也不能選(D)。

3.女子要做什麼？

(A) 打一封信給蘇珊娜。

(B) 打一張公告。

(C) 完成案子。

(D) 帶派對帽來。

女子接下來或許也有可能要完成案子、或帶派對帽來公司，但在對話裡她並沒有提到，所以我們還是只能選(B)，因為她答應男子要打一張公告。

多益聽力搶分有祕密，全真模擬試題29

1. What is the man most likely doing?　　🎧 **Track 29**

   (A) Complaining to a friend about work.

   (B) Complaining to his sister about his boss.

   (C) Complaining to his boss about an assistant.

   (D) Complaining to his dog about his workload.

2. What is the problem with the new assistant?

   (A) She is too nosy.

   (B) She is often late.

   (C) She is a slow learner.

   (D) She is too loud.

3. What will the woman do?

   (A) Talk to the new assistant.

   (B) Fire the new assistant.

   (C) Find a new assistant.

   (D) Praise the new assistant.

GO ON TO THE NEXT PAGE

多益聽力搶分有祕密，
全真模擬試題-P127頁答案與詳解

題目解答

1. (C)   2. (B)   3. (A)

....

聽力原文

M: I don't mean to complain, but the new assistant isn't really doing her job. I mean, she's supposed to help us with office affairs, but no one can ever find her when we need her.

W: Really? I'm surprised; she seemed like a nice girl in the interview.

M: Appearances deceive, Ms. Wentworth! She has been late for three days straight, and even made a client wait for half^英 an hour.

W: That behavior is quite unacceptable. I'll give her a good talking-to later.

> **搶分重點**　❶ 口音為英國（男）與美國（女）。
> 　　　　　　❷ 英國腔中「half」的念法和美國腔不同。

聽力中譯

M：我不是想抱怨，可是新助理沒有做好的她的工作。我是說，她應該要幫我們處理辦公室事宜，可是我們需要她的時候總是找不到她。

W：真的嗎？我很驚訝，她面試的時候感覺真是個好女孩呢。

M：外表會騙人啊，文特沃司女士！她已經連三天遲到了，還害一個客戶等她半個小時呢。

W：這樣的行為實在難以接受。我待會會好好跟她聊聊。

聽力題目詳解

1. 男子很可能正在做什麼？

(A) 向朋友抱怨工作的事。

(B) 向姊妹抱怨老闆的事。

(C) **向老闆抱怨助理的事。**

(D) 向狗抱怨工作負擔的事。

多益聽力搶分有祕密，滿分高手10秒解題關鍵

只要能確認這段對話中女子的身分，就能夠回答這一題。從男子稱女子為「女士」看來，女子的地位應該比較高。而女子最後說要和助理好好談談，可見女子應該是有權力和員工「談談」的人，而男子不是，不然為什麼他自己不去和助理談呢？因此，可以判斷女子很可能是男子的老闆。(D)選項可以立刻剔除，因為雖然我們也可能會和狗抱怨事情，但狗一般是不會用人類的語言回答的，可知對話中的女子並非一隻狗。

---

2. 新助理有什麼問題？

(A) 她太多管閒事了。

(B) **她常遲到。**

(C) 她學得很慢。

(D) 她太吵了。

如果同事太吵、太多管閒事、學得很慢，的確都是問題，但男子並未指出助理有這些問題，只說她連續遲到幾天，還要客戶等她，可見要選(B)。

3. 女子會做什麼？

   (A) 和新助理談談。

   (B) 開除新助理。

   (C) 找一個新的助理。

   (D) 稱讚新助理。

女子最後說要找新助理談談，並未提及要開除她或另覓其他人選。而男子剛和她抱怨了這麼多，可知女子應該不會稱讚新助理，所以選(A)。

多益聽力搶分有祕密，全真模擬試題30

1. Why is the man asking for a day off?　　　🎧 **Track 30**

　(A) He is too tired to work.

　(B) He doesn't like Mrs. Emory.

　(C) He has a headache.

　(D) He wants to get a doctor's note.

2. What does the woman want the man to do?

　(A) Go home and rest.

　(B) Try not to get sick so often.

　(C) Write down his schedule.

　(D) Write the doctor a note.

3. What is true about the man?

　(A) Someone wants to kill him.

　(B) He wants to see a doctor.

　(C) He has a doctor's note.

　(D) He has not asked for a leave this month.

GO ON TO THE NEXT PAGE

多益聽力搶分有祕密，
全真模擬試題-P131頁答案與詳解

題目解答

1. (C)   2. (B)   3. (B)

聽力原文

M: Mrs. Emory, I would like to take a day off if it's all right with you.

W: But you've asked for leave 3 times this month already! And this month has barely even begun.

M: I know, but I really need to see the doctor. This headache is killing me. I can't concentrate on my work at all[英]!

W: All right, then. Don't forget to bring the doctor's note in tomorrow. Try not to get sick so often; we're on a tight schedule here!

> **搶分重點**
> ❶ 口音為英國（男）與美國（女）。
> ❷ 仔細聽聽男子的「at all」，發音是不是很特別呢？可以多聽幾次習慣一下。

聽力中譯

M：愛莫麗太太，我想請一天假，如果妳同意的話。

W：但你這個月已經請三次假了耶！而且這個月根本才剛開始。

M：我知道，但我真的得去看醫生。我頭快痛死了，完全沒辦法專心工作。

W：那好吧，別忘了明天要帶醫生的證明進來。試著不要這麼常生病吧，我們的行程可是排很緊的！

聽力題目詳解

1. 為什麼男子要請一天假？

    (A) 他累得無法工作。

    (B) 他不喜歡愛莫麗太太。

    (C) 他頭痛。

    (D) 他想拿醫生證明。

多益聽力搶分有祕密，滿分高手10秒解題關鍵

男子頭痛欲裂，想去看醫生，所以請假，和他疲累、或討厭女子沒有任何關係。而拿醫生證明是他去看醫生時要做的事情，他並非為了拿醫生證明而特別請假，所以選**(C)**。

---

2. 女子想要男子做什麼？

    (A) 回家休息。

    (B) 試著不要那麼常生病。

    (C) 寫下他的行程。

    (D) 寫一張字條給醫師。

多益聽力搶分有祕密，滿分高手10秒解題關鍵

女子要男子帶醫生寫的證明到公司，而非叫男子寫一張字條給醫師，所以不選**(D)**。此外，女子並沒有叫男子回家休息、或寫下行程，所以只能選擇**(B)**。

3. 關於男子，何者為真？

   (A) 有人想殺他。

   (B) 他想看醫生。

   (C) 他有醫生開的證明。

   (D) 他這個月不曾請假過。

多益聽力搶分有祕密，滿分高手10秒解題關鍵

這題要注意：This headache is killing me直翻就是「頭痛要殺死我了」，也就是頭痛得要死的意思。不要只聽到kill這個字，就認定有人想要殺了男子，而他因為被追殺而想請假。

多益聽力搶分有祕密，全真模擬試題31

1. What is the woman complaining about? 🎧 **Track 31**

   (A) The man.

   (B) Her coworker.

   (C) Her client.

   (D) The man's coworker.

2. Why does the woman say "poor girl"?

   (A) She thinks her client is poor.

   (B) Her client was afraid to talk to her coworkers.

   (C) Her client has a little girl.

   (D) Her client's coworkers are all girls.

3. What does the man tell the woman to do?

   (A) Talk to her client nicely.

   (B) Like her client more.

   (C) Ask her client some questions.

   (D) Solve her client's problems.

GO ON TO THE NEXT PAGE

多益聽力搶分有祕密，
全真模擬試題-P135頁答案與詳解

題目解答

1. (C)　　　　2. (B)　　　　3. (A)

聽力原文

W: Ugh, this client is impossible to talk to. She keeps bothering me with questions about her own company! Shouldn't she ask^澳 her own coworkers instead?

M: Oh, do you mean Jackie from Collins Software? She's been bothering me too. I'm under the impression that her coworkers don't like her, so she's afraid of asking^英 them questions.

W: Really? Poor girl! But we can't^澳 help her solve her problems.

M: Yeah. Maybe you should tell her very nicely that you can't^英 provide her the answers she wants.

> **搶分重點**
> ❶ 口音為英國（男）與澳洲（女）。
> ❷ 澳洲腔中的「ask」和英國腔很類似，母音都比較偏向長的「ㄚ」，和美國腔很不同。但有沒有發現呢？澳洲腔的「can't」又和英國腔的聽起來不一樣。

聽力中譯

W：唉，跟這個客戶講話超困難的，她一直問我她自己公司的問題耶！她不是應該問自己的同事才對嗎？

M：喔，妳說柯林斯軟體公司的潔姬嗎？她也有來煩我。我印象中好像是她的同事不喜歡她，所以她不敢問他們問題。

W：真的喔？可憐的女孩！但我們也沒辦法幫她解決問題啊。

M：對啊，妳或許應該很友善地跟她說妳無法提供她她要的答案。

聽力題目詳解

1. 女子在抱怨誰的事？

　　(A) 男子。

　　(B) 她同事。

　　(C) 她的客戶。

　　(D) 男子的同事。

多益聽力搶分有祕密，滿分高手10秒解題關鍵

有時一題的答案可以從其他題中看出一點端倪。在這裡我們發現後面的兩題都不斷提到女子的客戶，看來女子的客戶在這段對話裡一定經常出現。因此，我們可以在聽對話前就先猜個大概，女子很可能是在抱怨客戶的事喔！

---

2. 女子為什麼說「可憐的女孩」？

　　(A) 她覺得她的客戶很窮。

　　(B) 她的客戶不敢和同事說話。

　　(C) 她的客戶有個小女兒。

　　(D) 她的客戶的同事都是女孩。

男子和女子提到客戶不敢問自己的同事問題後，女子似乎很同情地說「可憐的女孩」，可見應該選(B)。選項(A)中的poor指的是「貧窮的」，和女子說的「poor girl」指的「可憐的」意思不同。注意，說「某人 + be動詞 + poor」這樣的句型時，poor絕對不會指「可憐的」，只能是「貧窮的」的意思喔！

3. 男子叫女子做什麼？

(A) 友善地和她的客戶談話。

(B) 更喜歡她的客戶一點。

(C) 問客戶一些問題。

(D) 解決客戶的問題。

一般工作時，都會希望能解決客戶的問題，但這個客戶的問題卻是她自己公司的事，是女子無法解決的，所以只能好好和她談了。答案是(A)。

多益聽力搶分有祕密，全真模擬試題32

1. Where are the man and woman?　　　🎧 **Track 32**

   (A) In the meeting room.

   (B) Waiting for their meals.

   (C) Beside the company restroom.

   (D) In front of their desks.

2. What is this discussion about?

   (A) How there are too few floors.

   (B) How men take too long using the restroom.

   (C) How hard work is.

   (D) How there too few restrooms.

3. What does the man suggest about men and women toilets?

   (A) They should be built together.

   (B) They should be separated.

   (C) They should be cleaner.

   (D) They should be closer to each other.

GO ON TO THE NEXT PAGE ➡

多益聽力搶分有祕密，
全真模擬試題-P139頁答案與詳解

題目解答

1. (C)　　　　2. (D)　　　　3. (B)

聽力原文

W: The restrooms sure are popular today.

M: I know! I'm actually considering bringing this up at the next company meeting. We can't survive on two restrooms for the whole floor.

W: Yeah, it's hard to get work done if you have to spend 20 minutes just waiting to use the restroom.

M: And they should separate men and women's toilets too. You ladies take forever[2] to come out!

> **搶分重點**
> [1] 口音為英國（男）與澳洲（女）。
> [2] 女生上廁所真的會花上「永遠」那麼久嗎？當然沒有，男子這麼說只是想開玩笑，所以在對話中也特別加重語氣強調了「forever」這個字，以表誇張。

聽力中譯

W： 廁所今天真熱門啊。

M： 我知道啊！我其實在考慮下次公司開會時提出這件事。我們不可能整層樓都靠兩間廁所過活啊。

W： 對啊，上個廁所都要等20分鐘，很難好好完成工作呢。

M： 應該也要把男廁跟女廁分開。妳們女生每次都好久才出來啊！

聽力題目詳解

1. 男子與女子在哪裡？

(A) 在會議室。

(B) 在等著上菜。

(C) 在公司的廁所旁。

(D) 在辦公桌前。

多益聽力搶分有祕密，滿分高手10秒解題關鍵

雖然兩人提到公司會議的事，但兩人並沒有真的正在開會。從女子所說「廁所真熱門」，可知他們位於一個「看得到廁所很熱門」的地方，那就是廁所附近了。兩人不是正在等著上廁所，就是經過廁所。

2. 這個對話是關於什麼？

(A) 樓層太少了。

(B) 男人上廁所上太久了。

(C) 工作太難了。

(D) 廁所太少了。

多益聽力搶分有祕密，滿分高手10秒解題關鍵

女子說「等上廁所就要等個20分鐘」，看來她的公司一定是廁所太少了，不然不會導致這樣的窘境。因此，要選(D)這個選項。

3. 關於男廁與女廁，男子有什麼建議？

   (A) 應該要一起蓋。

   (B) 應該要分開來。

   (C) 應該要乾淨一些。

   (D) 應該要蓋得近一點。

多益聽力搶分有祕密，滿分高手10秒解題關鍵

男子開玩笑地抱怨女人上廁所實在上太久了，可見他希望男廁女廁分開，才不會讓上廁所較快的男性在那邊乾等女性出來，所以選 (B)。

多益聽力搶分有祕密，全真模擬試題**33**

1. What does the woman ask the man to do?　　　🎧 **Track 33**

   (A) To show around a new coworker.

   (B) To bring her teabags.

   (C) To print something for her.

   (D) To wait for her till later.

2. What room might the company NOT have?

   (A) A restroom.

   (B) A printing room.

   (C) A mail room.

   (D) A dining room.

3. What can we infer about this company?

   (A) They provide free teabags.

   (B) They provide free lunch.

   (C) They are a technology company.

   (D) There is only one floor.

GO ON TO THE NEXT PAGE

多益聽力搶分有祕密，
全真模擬試題-P143頁答案與詳解

題目解答

1. (A)   2. (D)   3. (A)

聽力原文

W: Can you show Lydia around for a bit? Today is her first day.

M: My pleasure. But what places should I show her?

W: Well, there's the restroom, the printing room, the mail room, the corner where we provide free teabags, and the floor where the tech people can be found.

M: Okay. Should I also show her all our favorite places to have lunch?

W: That can wait until later!

> **搶分重點** 🔊 口音為英國（男）與澳洲（女）。

聽力中譯

W： 你可以帶麗迪雅到處看看嗎？她今天第一天來。

M： 我很樂意。但我要帶她去看哪些地方呢？

W： 嗯，廁所啦、影印室啦、放免費茶包的角落啦、郵件收發室啦、還有要找技術人員的時候要去的那層樓。

M： 好。我也要帶她去看我們最喜歡的午餐地點嗎？

W： 那個還是等一下吧！

聽力題目詳解

1. 女子請男子做什麼？

   (A) 帶新同事到處看看。

   (B) 帶茶包給她。

   (C) 幫她印東西。

   (D) 等她一下。

多益聽力搶分有祕密，滿分高手10秒解題關鍵

女子提到了公司內的許多地點，但並非要男子去這些地點幫她辦事，而是要他帶著新同事認識這些地方，所以選(A)。

---

2. 公司可能沒有哪一間？

   (A) 廁所。

   (B) 印刷室。

   (C) 郵件收發室。

   (D) 用餐室。

多益聽力搶分有祕密，滿分高手10秒解題關鍵

公司有用餐室雖然也不會不合理，但女子已經提到了其他三間，而沒有提到用餐室，所以只能選(D)了。聽到像女子這樣「列舉東西」的題目時，盡量趕快把每樣東西記下來，平常就可以請朋友隨機念幾個物品的名稱，練習如何在短時間內將列舉的項目記好。

3. 關於這個公司，我們可以知道哪些事項？

   (A) 他們有提供免費茶包。

   (B) 他們有提供免費午餐。

   (C) 他們是科技公司。

   (D) 只有一層樓。

多益聽力搶分有祕密，滿分高手10秒解題關鍵

女子提到有個角落擺放免費茶包，所以要選(A)。其中女子說過公司有一層樓可以找到「tech people」，這指的是技術人員，如公司有人電腦當機時就可以找這些人來修理。各種公司都有可能有技術人員，不代表這就是一家科技公司。

多益聽力搶分有祕密，全真模擬試題34

1. Who is Greg likely to be?　　　　　　　　🎧 **Track 34**

    (A) The man and woman's child.

    (B) The man and woman's coworker.

    (C) The man and woman's father.

    (D) The man and woman's online friend.

2. What does the woman want the man to do?

    (A) Not work overtime.

    (B) Finish the proposal.

    (C) Remember to lock the place.

    (D) Leave with her.

3. Why does the man not want to leave yet?

    (A) He has a proposal to finish.

    (B) He does not want to lock up the place.

    (C) He wants to lock people out.

    (D) He wants to overwork.

GO ON TO THE NEXT PAGE

多益聽力搶分有祕密，
全真模擬試題-P147頁答案與詳解

題目解答

1. **(B)**   2. **(C)**   3. **(A)**

聽力原文

W: It's late. Aren't you leaving?

M: Not yet. I've got to finish this proposal first.

W: Okay^澳 then. Just remember to lock up the place when you go, and bring the key with you. Last time Greg worked overtime, he locked us all out the next day.

M: I remember that. I'll be careful.

W: Good. I'm off then! Don't overwork yourself!

> **搶分重點**
> ❶ 口音為英國（男）與澳洲（女）。
> ❷ 注意澳洲口音中發「okay」的「o」時，聽起來是不是和我們平常講的「OK」聽起來很不一樣呢？

聽力中譯

W： 很晚了耶，你不走嗎？

M： 還不行，我要先完成這個提案。

W： 好吧。離開前要記得鎖門喔，然後要帶鑰匙。上次葛瑞格加班的時候，隔天把我們通通鎖在外面了。

M： 我記得那次。我會小心。

W： 好，那我走囉！不要工作太累啊！

聽力題目詳解

1. 葛瑞格可能是誰？

    (A) 男子與女子的孩子。

    (B) 男子與女子的同事。

    (C) 男子與女子的父親。

    (D) 男子與女子的網友。

多益聽力搶分有祕密，滿分高手10秒解題關鍵

一旦發現題目中有出現名字（如這題的Greg），就必須在聽對話時張大耳朵仔細找這個名字，因為兩人在對話中或許只會提到他一次，錯過了就沒機會了，尤其是像Greg這種單音節很短的名字更是。這裡女子說Greg上次加班把大家鎖在外面，應該就能判斷他是男子與女子的同事。

---

2. 女子要男子做什麼？

    (A) 不要加班。

    (B) 完成提案。

    (C) 記得鎖門。

    (D) 和她一起離開。

得知男子要加班後，女子沒有強迫他跟她一起下班，而是要他記得鎖門，並拿鑰匙，所以要選(C)。女子或許也可能希望男子完成提案，但她並沒有說出來，所以不可選(B)。

3. 為什麼男子還不想走？

(A) 他要完成提案。

(B) 他不想鎖門。

(C) 他想把大家鎖在外面。

(D) 他想工作過度。

最後一個選項中的overwork指的是「工作過量、疲勞過度」的意思，而非「加班」（想說「加班」則可改說work overtime）。因此，這題可別誤以為(D)要說的是「他想加班」而選擇了這個答案！

多益聽力搶分有祕密，全真模擬試題35

1. What are the man and woman doing?　　　🎧 **Track 35**

　　(A) They are shopping together.

　　(B) They are negotiating prices.

　　(C) They are chatting on the phone.

　　(D) They are looking for the man's boss.

2. What is true about the man?

　　(A) He agrees to give the woman a 10% discount.

　　(B) He will place some orders in the following 8 months.

　　(C) He wants to talk to his boss before he makes a decision.

　　(D) He agrees to sign a contract.

3. Why does the woman want the man to lower the price?

　　(A) Because it is beyond their budget.

　　(B) Because she wants to place more orders.

　　(C) Because her orders are larger.

　　(D) Because she wants to talk to her boss first.

GO ON TO THE NEXT PAGE

多益聽力搶分有祕密，
全真模擬試題-P151頁答案與詳解

題目解答

1. (B)   2. (C)   3. (A)

聽力原文

W: Your price is beyond our budget. Won't you consider giving us a 10 percent discount?

M: Sorry, this is really the best price that we can offer.

W: Would you consider lowering the price if we promise to place several large orders in the following eight months?

M: Hmm, that doesn't sound too bad of a deal. Let me think it over. I'll have to talk^英 to my boss first.

搶分重點
- ❶ 口音為英國（男）與澳洲（女）。
- ❷ 仔細聽聽男子的「talk」，母音的發音方式和美國腔相當不同。

聽力中譯

W：您的價格是我們預算付不起的，你們願不願意考慮給我們打個九折？

M：抱歉啦，我們最低價真的只能這樣了。

W：如果我們保證接下來的八個月內會大批訂貨好幾次，你們願意降價嗎？

M：嗯，這交易聽起來好像不錯，讓我想想。我得先跟我老闆談談。

聽力題目詳解

1. 男子與女子在做什麼？

   (A) 他們正一起逛街。

   (B) 他們正在議價。

   (C) 他們正在用電話聊天。

   (D) 他們正在找男子的老闆。

多益聽力搶分有祕密，滿分高手10秒解題關鍵

這整段對話仔細一聽，兩人談的不外乎是「再便宜一點」之類的內容，可知他們很可能是在議價，所以選(B)。這段對話也可能是以電話進行，但(C)選項中提到兩人是在用電話「聊天」，而兩人聽起來並非在聊天，所以選(C)是不對的。

2. 有關男子，何者為真？

   (A) 他同意給女子打九折。

   (B) 他會在接下來八個月之內下幾次訂單。

   (C) 他想跟老闆談談再做決定。

   (D) 他同意簽合約。

多益聽力搶分有祕密，滿分高手10秒解題關鍵

整段對話中，男子雖然表示覺得女子的提議不錯，但並沒有對女子做出任何承諾，更別提簽什麼合約了，所以只能選(C)，想跟老闆談談再做決定。

3. 女子為什麼要男子降價？

    (A) 因為超過他們的預算。

    (B) 因為她想下更多訂單。

    (C) 因為她的訂單比較大。

    (D) 因為她想先和老闆聊聊。

多益聽力搶分有祕密，滿分高手10秒解題關鍵

女子一開口就說「不能降價嗎？我們的預算付不起」（Your price is beyond our budget. Won't you consider giving us a 10 percent discount?），可知女子希望男子降價是預算的關係，後面提到的「訂單」都是討價還價的過程中用的招數，並不是這題該選的選項。

多益聽力搶分有祕密，全真模擬試題36

1. Why does the woman want the man's email address?

   (A) She likes koalas.　　　　　　　　　🎧 **Track 36**

   (B) She wants to forward something to him.

   (C) She is changing computers.

   (D) She needs it for a survey.

2. What is true about the survey?

   (A) Customers care more about prices.

   (B) Customers care more about quality.

   (C) Customers have to fill in their email address.

   (D) It is about computers.

3. Which statement below is false?

   (A) The man's email address has the word "koala" in it.

   (B) The woman will forward the survey results to the man.

   (C) The man wants to see the survey results.

   (D) The woman thinks that the survey was pointless.

GO ON TO THE NEXT PAGE ➡

多益聽力搶分有祕密，
全真模擬試題-P155頁答案與詳解

題目解答

1. **(B)**　　　　2. **(B)**　　　　3. **(D)**

聽力原文

W: The results of the survey we did last week were pretty interesting. I didn't realize our customers cared so much more about quality than about price.

M: Oh, the results are out? Can you forward them to me?

W: Yep. Hey, wait, I think I lost your email last time I switched computers. Do you mind giving it to me again?

M: Not at all. It's koalasteve@kmail.com.

W: Thanks. I didn't know you liked koalas.

搶分重點 🔊 口音為英國（男）與澳洲（女）。

聽力中譯

W：我們上禮拜做的意見調查結果還蠻有趣的。我都不知道我們的消費者原來比起價格更在意品質呢。

M：喔，結果出來了喔？可以轉寄給我嗎？

W：好啊。喂，等等，我想我上次換電腦的時候把你的電子郵件地址弄丟了。你介意再給我一次嗎？

M：不介意。是koalasteve@kmail.com。

W：謝了。我都不知道你喜歡無尾熊呢。

聽力題目詳解

1. 女子為什麼要男子的電子郵件地址？

(A) 她喜歡無尾熊。

(B) 她想轉寄東西給他。

(C) 她正在換電腦。

(D) 意見調查需要用到。

多益聽力搶分有祕密，滿分高手10秒解題關鍵

這段對話的主題轉換得很快，從「意見調查」到「轉寄信」到「電子郵件帳號不見」到「喜歡無尾熊」，感覺好像很嚇人，但不必太過緊張，只要能掌握前因後果，跟上這個脈絡就沒有問題了，畢竟我們平常聊天的主題不也都是跳來跳去的嗎？這題中女子是因為要轉寄東西才和男子要電子郵件，所以選(B)。

---

2. 關於意見調查，何者為真？

(A) 消費者比較在意價格。

(B) 消費者比較在意品質。

(C) 消費者必須填電子郵件地址。

(D) 這是和電腦有關的意見調查。

女子只提到了有意見調查，但意外地整段對話中都沒有提到到底是「什麼產品」的意見調查。但因為女子所説的話，我們倒是知道<u>無論是什麼產品，總之消費者就是比較在意品質</u>，所以選**(B)**。

3. 下列哪個選項不為真？

(A) 男子的電子郵件地址中有「無尾熊」這個字。

(B) 女子會把意見調查的結果轉寄給男子。

(C) 男子想看意見調查的結果。

(D) 女子認為意見調查沒有意義。

女子認為意見調查的結果「非常有趣」（pretty interesting），還提到裡面令她意想不到的部分，可見女子並不會覺得這次意見調查沒有意義，所以**(D)**選項不為真，要選擇這個。

多益聽力搶分有祕密，全真模擬試題37

1. What does the woman most likely sell?　　🎧 **Track 37**

　　(A) Books.

　　(B) Clothes.

　　(C) Phones.

　　(D) Pens.

2. What does the man think regarding some of the products?

　　(A) They have potential to become popular.

　　(B) They are not very unique.

　　(C) They come in too many colors.

　　(D) They should be well-received by older people.

3. What does the woman think is the main strength of the products?

　　(A) The pretty colors.

　　(B) The innovative design.

　　(C) The simple interface.

　　(D) The responsive controls.

GO ON TO THE NEXT PAGE ➤

多益聽力搶分有祕密，
全真模擬試題-P159頁答案與詳解

題目解答

1. (C)　　　　　2. (A)　　　　　3. (B)

聽力原文

W: Would you like to look at some of our new products? Here's the catalogue.

M: Sure. Are these models the ones you released this month? They look quite unique.

W: Thank you. We pride ourselves on our innovative design.

M: I think these phones have the potential to be quite popular among younger people. Are these the only colors you have?

W: We have plans of releasing pink and green versions if this model is well received.

搶分重點
❶ 口音為英國（男）與澳洲（女）。
❷ 英國腔中「only」的念法和美國腔不同。

聽力中譯

W：您想看看我們的一些新產品嗎？型錄在這裡。

M：好啊。這些是你們這個月推出的型號嗎？看起來蠻特別的。

W：謝謝。我們以我們創新的設計為傲。

M：我認為這些手機有潛力受到年輕人歡迎。你們只有這些顏色嗎？

W：如果這個型號受歡迎，我們計畫再推出粉紅色與綠色的版本。

聽力題目詳解

1. 女子最可能賣什麼？

   (A) 書本。

   (B) 衣服。

   (C) 手機。

   (D) 原子筆。

多益聽力搶分有祕密，滿分高手10秒解題關鍵

男子在看型錄時，說「這手機有潛力受到年輕人歡迎」，可知女子賣的八九不離十是手機一類的3C產品，因此可將其他選項剔除。雖然兩人說到model可能也是模特兒的意思，但「the models you released this month」這句若解釋成「本月新推出的模特兒」似乎很奇怪，可知這裡的model指的是「型號」，所以產品當然也和服裝無關了。

---

2. 關於一些產品，男子的想法如何？

   (A) 它們有受歡迎的潛力。

   (B) 它們不太獨特。

   (C) 它們顏色太多了。

   (D) 它們應該會很受年紀較大的人歡迎。

多益聽力搶分有祕密，滿分高手10秒解題關鍵

男子認為產品很獨特，會受到年輕人歡迎，並詢問有沒有更多顏色，可見在這四個選項中刪來刪去也只能選(A)了。

3. 女子認為產品主要的優勢是什麼？

(A) 漂亮的顏色。

(B) 創新的設計。

(C) 簡單好用的介面。

(D) 反應快速的控制。

多益聽力搶分有祕密，滿分高手10秒解題關鍵

女子提到「我們最得意的就是創新的設計」（We pride ourselves on our innovative design），可知她認為他們公司的產品應該是以創新設計為主打。女子沒有稱讚產品的顏色，所以無法選(A)，而整個對話中並沒有提到介面、控制等事，因此也不可能選(C)或(D)。

多益聽力搶分有祕密，全真模擬試題38

1. What do we know about the woman?　　　　🎧 **Track 38**

(A) She is a seller of light bulbs.

(B) She is juggling seven projects.

(C) She just opened a box of light bulbs.

(D) She wants to call the man to complain.

2. What do we know about the man?

(A) He bought some light bulbs.

(B) He dropped the box.

(C) He called the delivery company.

(D) He is very busy.

3. Why is the woman complaining?

(A) The light bulbs are all shattered.

(B) The man won't listen.

(C) The man has too many projects.

(D) The man dropped the box.

GO ON TO THE NEXT PAGE ▶

多益聽力搶分有祕密，
全真模擬試題-P163頁答案與詳解

題目解答

1. (C)   2. (D)   3. (A)

聽力原文

W: Oh, my! The light bulbs that just arrived are all shattered!

M: What? You didn't drop the box again, did you?

W: Of course not. They were already like this when I opened the box. You should call the delivery company to complain.

M: Wait, why me? Why don't you just call them instead? I'm juggling seven projects at the same time already.

> **搶分重點**
>
> 🔎 口音為英國（男）與澳洲（女）。
>
> 🔎 男子在這裡的「you」特別加了重音，這是因為他的工作忙碌，認為打電話給貨運公司的事不該是他來做，而應該是女子來做，所以他強調「you」這個字，就是要告訴女子「應該是『妳』打這通電話才對吧」。

聽力中譯

W：唉呀！剛送到的燈泡都破了。

M：啊？妳不會又摔到箱子了吧？

W：當然沒有。我打開箱子的時候就已經這樣了。你應該打給運送公司抗議。

M：等等，為什麼是我啊？妳幹嘛不自己打？我現在同時有七個案子要處理耶。

聽力題目詳解

1. 有關女子，我們知道什麼事？

(A) 她是賣燈泡的。

(B) 她有七個案子要處理。

(C) 她剛打開了一箱燈泡。

(D) 她想打給男子抗議。

多益聽力搶分有祕密，滿分高手10秒解題關鍵

女子在對話開始時，發現燈泡都破了，還說她一打開箱子就發現是
這樣，可見她應該是剛打開裝燈泡的箱子，所以選(C)。女子可能
是賣燈泡的，也可能有很多案子要處理，但對話中她並沒有提到，
所以無法選這些選項。

2. 關於男子，我們知道什麼事？

(A) 他買了一些燈泡。

(B) 他把箱子摔了。

(C) 他打給運輸公司。

(D) 他很忙。

多益聽力搶分有祕密，滿分高手10秒解題關鍵

男子說他有七件案子要處理，連打個電話給貨運公司都沒空，看來
他現在應該是忙到不行，所以選(D)。

3. 女子為什麼在抱怨呢？

   (A) 燈泡都碎裂了。

   (B) 男子都不聽她講話。

   (C) 男子的案子太多了。

   (D) 男子把箱子摔了。

多益聽力搶分有祕密，全真模擬試題39

1. Which of the following statements is true?　　🎧 **Track 39**

   (A) It is currently December.

   (B) The man and woman are getting married.

   (C) Daniel and his girlfriend have dated for a long time.

   (D) The woman's wedding is in December.

2. What are the two talking about?

   (A) A colleague's wedding.

   (B) The woman's date.

   (C) The man's salary.

   (D) Birthday gifts.

3. What do we know about the woman?

   (A) She never complained.

   (B) She had a huge monthly bonus.

   (C) She likes to plan ahead.

   (D) She has a girlfriend of 12 years.

GO ON TO THE NEXT PAGE ➤

多益聽力搶分有祕密，
全真模擬試題-P167頁答案與詳解

題目解答

1. (C)   2. (A)   3. (C)

聽力原文

W: Hey! Have you heard? Daniel's finally proposed to his girlfriend. They're getting married early December!

M: Finally? After dating for 12 years? Took him long enough.

W: I know! I can't believe his girlfriend never complained. Anyway, do you have any ideas for wedding gifts? The whole department should pool our monthly bonuses and get him something nice.

M: It's only January and you're planning already?

搶分重點 🔊 口音為英國（男）與澳洲（女）。

聽力中譯

W：喂！你聽説了嗎？丹尼爾終於對他女友求婚了。他們十二月初要結婚了！

M：終於啊？在一起都12年了耶？他也拖夠久了。

W：我知道啊！我真難相信他女友都沒抗議。總之，你有什麼婚禮禮物有關的主意嗎？整個部門應該把月終獎金湊一湊，買點好東西給他才對。

M：現在才一月耶，妳就在計畫了？

聽力題目詳解

1. 以下哪一句是正確的？

(A) 現在是十二月。

(B) 男子與女子要結婚了。

(C) 丹尼爾和他女友已經在一起很久了。

(D) 女子的婚禮在十二月。

多益聽力搶分有祕密，滿分高手10秒解題關鍵

兩人談論的是別人的婚禮，並非男子或女子的婚禮，可知不能選
(B)或(D)。此外，男子提到現在是一月，所以(A)選項也不對，(C)
才是正確的。

....

2. 兩人在講什麼？

(A) 同事的婚禮。

(B) 女子的約會。

(C) 男子的薪水。

(D) 生日禮物。

多益聽力搶分有祕密，滿分高手10秒解題關鍵

雖然兩人有提到「禮物」，但講的是同事結婚要送他的禮物，而非
生日禮物。正確的答案是(A)。

3. 關於女子，我們知道什麼事？

(A) 她從來不抱怨。

(B) 她的月底獎金額很高。

(C) 她喜歡提早計畫。

(D) 她有已經交往12年的女友。

多益聽力搶分有祕密，滿分高手10秒解題關鍵

現在明明是一月，女子卻在計畫十二月的事，連要同事們一起把月底的獎金拿來湊都想好了，可知她這個人非常喜歡提早計畫事情。Plan ahead這個片語指的就是在事情發生前早先做好計畫的意思。

多益聽力搶分有祕密，全真模擬試題40

1. What is the man doing?　　　　　　　　🎧 **Track 40**

　　(A) He is helping the woman pick out a dress.

　　(B) He is interviewing the woman.

　　(C) He is buying the woman a bag.

　　(D) He is organizing a folder for the woman.

2. Why does the woman think there is an emergency?

　　(A) Her house is on fire.

　　(B) She is late for the interview.

　　(C) She can't find the right thing to wear.

　　(D) She lost her bag.

3. What does the man advise the woman to do?

　　(A) Bring a bag.

　　(B) Be confident.

　　(C) Wear a white dress.

　　(D) Love the man.

GO ON TO THE NEXT PAGE

多益聽力搶分有祕密，
全真模擬試題-P171頁答案與詳解

題目解答

1. **(A)**   2. **(C)**   3. **(B)**

聽力原文

W: This is an emergency! I can't find the right dress for my interview!

M: Relax, I'm right here to help. Hmm, how about this sleek black dress? It's elegant, and the material makes you look all brisk and serious.

W: But I don't have a bag that goes^澳 with it!

M: Don't bring a bag then. Just carry a professional-looking folder and stride in like you own the place. They'll love you!

> **搶分重點**
> ❶ 口音為英國（男）與澳洲（女）。
> ❷ 澳洲腔中的「goes」念法和我們習慣的美國腔不大一樣。

聽力中譯

W：現在事態很緊急！我找不到適合面試穿的洋裝！

M：放輕鬆，我來幫妳。嗯，這件俐落的黑色洋裝怎樣？很高雅，材質讓妳看起來既有效率又認真。

W：可是我沒有包包可以搭啊！

M：那就別帶包包，只要拿個看起來很專業的文件夾，大方地像回自己家一樣走進去就行了！他們一定會很喜歡妳！

聽力題目詳解

1. 男子在做什麼？

   (A) 他在幫女子挑洋裝。

   (B) 他在面試女子。

   (C) 他在買包包給女子。

   (D) 他在為女子整理資料夾。

多益聽力搶分有祕密，滿分高手10秒解題關鍵

從這個對話中應該可以聽出一個情境：女子要面試，嚷著沒東西可穿，於是男子身為她的閨中密友，就義不容辭地提供專業建議。一旦瞭解了這個電影中似乎常出現的情境，接下來的問題應該就都很好答了。

2. 女子為什麼覺得事態緊急？

   (A) 她家火災了。

   (B) 她面試遲到了。

   (C) 她找不到合適的東西可以穿。

   (D) 她的包包不見了。

多益聽力搶分有祕密，滿分高手10秒解題關鍵

Emergency 在對話中指的不見得都是火災、急診等等嚴重的事，也有可能是誇張說法，故意將小事說得很可怕。女子在這裡就是這樣，不過是找不到衣服，就說是緊急事態，不用一聽到emergency就覺得發生意外，需要急救。

3. 男子建議女子做什麼？

   (A) 帶包包。

   (B) 有信心。

   (C) 穿白色洋裝。

   (D) 愛上男子。

多益聽力搶分有祕密，全真模擬試題41

1. Where does the man work on Saturdays?　　🎧 **Track 41**

   (A) At school.

   (B) At a burger place.

   (C) At the woman's place.

   (D) At a hairdresser's.

2. Why does the man suggest the woman work at his workplace?

   (A) She can introduce him.

   (B) She can focus on her studies.

   (C) She is his type.

   (D) She can talk to the guy she likes.

3. What do we know about Ryan?

   (A) He works on Saturdays.

   (B) He is light-haired.

   (C) He is petite.

   (D) He is quitting his job.

GO ON TO THE NEXT PAGE ➡

多益聽力搶分有祕密，
全真模擬試題-P175頁答案與詳解

題目解答

1. (B)　　　　　2. (D)　　　　　3. (A)

聽力原文

W: That guy who works with you at the burger joint on Saturdays is really my type. Do you think you can introduce me next time?

M: Oh, you mean Ryan? The tall guy with dark hair? I would love to introduce you, but I'm quitting my job next week to focus on my studies, so...

W: Aw, that's too bad.

M: Wait, I've got an idea. We'll be a bit understaffed once I leave, so you can apply to work there and you'll be able to talk to Ryan all ^英 day!

> **搶分重點**
> ❶ 口音為英國（男）與澳洲（女）。
> ❷ 英國腔中的「all」念法和我們習慣的美國腔不大一樣。

聽力中譯

W： 星期六跟你一起在漢堡店工作的男生真是我喜歡的型。你下次可以介紹我們認識嗎？

M： 喔，妳說萊恩嗎？高個子、深色頭髮的那個？我是很想幫妳介紹啦，可是我要專心於學業，下禮拜就要辭職了，所以……

W： 是喔，那就太可惜了。

M： 等一下，我有個好點子。我離開以後我們就會有點人手不足，所以妳可以申請到那裡工作，這樣妳就整天都可以和萊恩聊天啦！

聽力題目詳解

1. 男子在星期六在哪工作？

(A) 學校。

(B) 漢堡店。

(C) 女子家。

(D) 理髮店。

多益聽力搶分有祕密，滿分高手10秒解題關鍵

男子在對話中雖提到他很快就要從漢堡店辭職了，但<u>他現在畢竟還
沒辭職，所以還是算是漢堡店的員工，因此選(B)</u>。

2.男子為何建議女子在他工作的地方工作？

(A) 她可以介紹他。

(B) 她可以專注於學業。

(C) 她是他喜歡的型。

(D) 她可以跟她喜歡的男生講話。

多益聽力搶分有祕密，滿分高手10秒解題關鍵

男子建議女子在他辭職後接下他的工作，一方面是忠誠地擔心老闆
找不到新人、人手不夠，一方面也是給女子製造機會，<u>讓她跟心
儀的對象認識</u>。這裡沒有「人手不足」的選項，因此我們只能選
(D)。

3. 關於萊恩，我們知道什麼事？

   (A) 他在星期六工作。

   (B) 他的頭髮是淺色的。

   (C) 他個子嬌小。

   (D) 他要辭職了。

多益聽力搶分有祕密，滿分高手10秒解題關鍵

男子提到萊恩有著深色頭髮、個子很高，而女子也提到萊恩和男子一起在星期六在漢堡店工作。從這些資訊，我們很快能對萊恩有基本的瞭解，也能排除不對的選項，選擇正確的(A)。

多益聽力搶分有祕密，全真模擬試題42

1. Why is the woman avoiding the man?　　　🎧 **Track 42**

    (A) She is scared of him.

    (B) She is angry at him.

    (C) She feels guilty.

    (D) She feels annoyed.

2. What is true about the man?

    (A) He got assigned to the client of his dreams.

    (B) He did research on a company.

    (C) He is mad at the woman.

    (D) He did something wrong.

3. How does the woman feel about the client she was assigned to?

    (A) She is happy to work with them.

    (B) She is frightened of them.

    (C) She wishes the man could work with them.

    (D) She did research on them.

GO ON TO THE NEXT PAGE

多益聽力搶分有祕密，
全真模擬試題-P179頁答案與詳解

題目解答

1. (C)　　　　2. (B)　　　　3. (C)

聽力原文

M: Why have you been avoiding me these days? What did I do wrong?

W: Nothing. I guess it's because I feel guilty that I got assigned the client you wanted to work with.

M: What? Just because of that? But that's not your fault. You can't decide what client you get assigned to.

W: I know, but I also know that you had been doing research on their company and really wanted to work with them, so it feels like I stole your client from you.

> **搶分重點**　🔊 口音為英國（男）與澳洲（女）。

聽力中譯

M：妳最近為什麼一直在躲我呢？我做錯什麼了？

W：沒什麼。我想是因為我覺得很有罪惡感，因為我被分配到你想合作的客戶。

M：什麼？就因為這樣？那又不是妳的錯。妳不能決定妳被分配到哪個客戶啊。

W：我知道，可是我也知道你一直在蒐集他們公司的資訊，很想和他們合作，所以我感覺好像我搶了你的客戶。

聽力題目詳解

1. 女子為什麼在躲男子？

    (A) 她怕他。

    (B) 她生他的氣。

    (C) 她覺得有罪惡感。

    (D) 她覺得很煩。

多益聽力搶分有祕密，滿分高手**10**秒解題關鍵

女子覺得自己搶了男子的客戶，很對不起他，因此有罪惡感，才避開男子不和他説話，並非男子惹她生氣或讓她害怕。因此選(B)。

2. 有關男子，何者為真？

    (A) 他被分配到他夢想合作的客戶。

    (B) 他收集了一家公司的資料。

    (C) 他對女子生氣。

    (D) 他做錯事了。

多益聽力搶分有祕密，滿分高手**10**秒解題關鍵

男子對和某個客戶合作非常有興趣，因此積極地蒐集那家公司的資料，因此選(B)。整段對話中，男子其實並沒有提到他自己的事，所以必須仔細聽女子如何形容男子，才能判斷到底該選哪一個答案。

3. 女子對於她被分配到的客戶有什麼感覺？

(A) 她樂於與他們合作。

(B) 她害怕他們。

(C) 她希望男子能與他們合作。

(D) 她收集了和他們相關的資料。

多益聽力搶分有祕密，滿分高手10秒解題關鍵

女子之所以這麼有罪惡感，是因為她覺得應該要是男子和她的客戶合作才對，不該是她，所以(C)選項最能夠形容她的心情。

多益聽力搶分有祕密，全真模擬試題43

1. Where are the man and woman?   🎧 **Track 43**

   (A) On a train.

   (B) On a plane.

   (C) On a bus.

   (D) On a ship.

2. How do the man and woman feel about the turbulence?

   (A) They are very frightened.

   (B) They think it is fun.

   (C) They are not bothered at all.

   (D) They think it's troublesome because they can't sleep.

3. What is true about the man?

   (A) He will be attending a conference.

   (B) He is on vacation.

   (C) He sleeps soundly when traveling.

   (D) He thinks the woman is disturbing him.

GO ON TO THE NEXT PAGE ➡

多益聽力搶分有祕密，
全真模擬試題-P183頁答案與詳解

題目解答

1. (B)　　　　　　2. (D)　　　　　　3. (A)

聽力原文

M: The flight is quite bumpy today, isn't it?

W: Yeah, I can't sleep because of all the turbulence.

M: Neither can I, which is pretty bad because I have an important conference to attend 3 hours after we arrive, and I need to be in tip-top condition!

W: Wow, that sounds exhausting. I'm glad I get to do some sightseeing for a couple of days before getting to work-related stuff.

搶分重點
　口音為英國（男）與澳洲（女）。
　neither這個字的第一個音節，有些人會唸類似「尼」的音，有些人會唸類似「耐」的音，依個人習慣不同。「either」這個字也是這樣。

聽力中譯

M：今天飛機很晃啊，不是嗎？

W：對啊，搖成這樣我都不能睡了。

M：我也是，這還蠻糟的，因為我們抵達三個小時後我就得去參加重要的研討會，一定要以最佳狀態出席才行。

W：哇，聽起來真累。幸好我可以觀光個幾天再處理工作的事務。

聽力題目詳解

1. 男子與女子在哪裡？

    (A) 火車上。

    (B) 飛機上。

    (C) 公車上。

    (D) 船上。

多益聽力搶分有祕密，滿分高手10秒解題關鍵

從兩人提到「flight」（飛航）與「turbulence」（氣流不穩）這些關鍵字可以判斷兩人應該是在飛機上。如果是在陸地上或海上，比較可能會說「the ride is bumpy」而非「the flight is bumpy」。

2. 男子與女子對氣流不穩有什麼感覺？

    (A) 他們非常害怕。

    (B) 他們覺得很好玩。

    (C) 他們一點都不在意。

    (D) 他們覺得很麻煩，因為睡不著。

多益聽力搶分有祕密，滿分高手10秒解題關鍵

有些幸運的人一上飛機就會不省人事，怎樣搖都搖不起來，但顯然兩人並不是如此。他們聽起來相當平靜，可知他們並非害怕氣流不穩，而只是因為睡不著了而有點困擾。

3. 關於男子，何者為真？

   (A) 他要參加研討會。

   (B) 他在放假。

   (C) 他在旅行時睡得很熟。

   (D) 他覺得女子打擾到他了。

多益聽力搶分有祕密，滿分高手10秒解題關鍵

男子提到接下來要參加研討會，可知他並不是因為放假才搭飛機出去玩，是有正事要辦。正確的答案應該選(A)。

多益聽力搶分有祕密，全真模擬試題44

1. Where did the man and woman run into each other?

   (A) In the woman's office. 　　　　　🎧 **Track 44**

   (B) In the post office.

   (C) At the Human Resources department.

   (D) On the street.

2. Why are the man and woman not working at their desks?

   (A) They are slacking off.

   (B) It is raining.

   (C) They have errands to run.

   (D) They are having a drive.

3. What did the man give the woman a ride?

   (A) On his car.

   (B) It is raining.

   (C) He left his umbrella in his office.

   (D) He is slacking off.

GO ON TO THE NEXT PAGE

多益聽力搶分有祕密，
全真模擬試題-P187頁答案與詳解

題目解答

1. (D)　　　　　2. (C)　　　　　3. (B)

聽力原文

M: Hey, Sonya, why are you walking in the rain? Want a ride?

W: Yes! Thank you so much! I came out to post a few letters and it started pouring out of nowhere! I left my umbrella in the office.

M: You're lucky you ran into me then.

W: What are you doing driving outside though? You can get fired if they catch you slacking off.

M: I'm not slacking off!② I'm just delivering a package for Tina from Human Resources.

> **搶分重點**
> ① 口音為英國（男）與澳洲（女）。
> ② 男子為什麼會特別加重音說「slacking off」兩個字呢？這是因為他覺得莫名其妙被指控偷懶很無理，所以特別以咬牙切齒的方式說，以表示自己想也沒想過要偷懶。

聽力中譯

M：喂，索妮雅，妳為什麼在雨中走？要我載妳一程嗎？

W：要！太謝謝你了！我出來寄幾封信，結果就莫名其妙下起大雨了。我把雨傘放在辦公室了。

M：那真是幸好妳遇到我呢。

W：不過你在外面開車做什麼？如果他們逮到你偷懶，會開除你的喔。

M：我沒在偷懶！我只是去幫人資部的提娜送個包裹而已。

聽力題目詳解

1. 男子與女子在哪裡遇到？

(A) 在女子的辦公室裡。

(B) 在郵局裡。

(C) 在人資部門。

(D) 在街上。

多益聽力搶分有祕密，滿分高手10秒解題關鍵

我們知道外面在下雨，女子在雨中行走，而男子開車經過，讓她搭一程。雖然我們不能完全確定這個對話發生在哪裡，但總之一定是室外，因為室內不會下雨，因此我們可以剔除所有室內的選項，選(D)。

---

2. 男子與女子為什麼沒有在辦公桌前工作？

(A) 他們在打混。

(B) 下雨了。

(C) 他們在跑腿。

(D) 他們在開車。

女子在上班時間出去寄信（由她問男子為什麼偷懶在外面開車可知現在是上班時間），但她說得理直氣壯的，可知她應該不是寄私人信件，而是寄公事上的信件。而男子說在替人資部的同事送包裹，可知女子和男子應該都是在「跑腿」，所以選(C)。

3. 男子為什麼載女子一程？

    (A) 在他的車上。

    (B) 在下雨。

    (C) 他把雨傘放在辦公室。

    (D) 他在偷懶。

「偷懶」和「在車上」都不構成載女子的理由，而把雨傘放在辦公室的人是女子而非男子，所以只能選(B)。

多益聽力搶分有祕密，全真模擬試題45

1. What is true about the woman? 　　　　🎧 **Track 45**

   (A) She wants to become an interior designer.

   (B) She is going to work in Korea.

   (C) She enjoys Thai food.

   (D) She will leave for Japan next week.

2. Why are the man and woman excited?

   (A) The woman will be studying abroad.

   (B) The woman got the internship she wanted.

   (C) The man will be studying abroad.

   (D) The man got the internship he wanted.

3. If this conversation were to have a title, which would be better?

   (A) Some Great News.

   (B) Excellent Food.

   (C) Interior Design Tips.

   (D) Blast It Open.

GO ON TO THE NEXT PAGE

多益聽力搶分有祕密，
全真模擬試題-P191頁答案與詳解

題目解答

1. **(A)**　　　　　2. **(B)**　　　　　3. **(A)**

聽力原文

W: I got that internship in Tokyo that I really wanted!

M: Great! When are you leaving for Japan?

W: Next month. I'm so excited! I'm sure it will be a blast. I can't wait to try all my favorite Japanese food.

M: Um, you're supposed to focus on your work, not the food! But congratulations anyway, this could help your future career as an interior designer a lot.

搶分重點　🔊 口音為英國（男）與澳洲（女）。

聽力中譯

W：我拿到我超想要的那個東京的實習機會了！

M：太棒了！妳什麼時候出發去日本？

W：下個月。我好興奮！我很確定會很棒的。我已經等不及試吃所有我最愛的日本料理了。

M：呃，妳應該要專心工作，而不是專心吃吧！不過還是恭喜了，這對妳未來成為室內設計師會很有幫助的。

聽力題目詳解

1. 關於女子，何者為真？

    (A) 她想成為室內設計師。

    (B) 她要在韓國工作。

    (C) 她喜歡泰國菜。

    (D) 她下週要去日本。

多益聽力搶分有祕密，滿分高手10秒解題關鍵

男子最後提到女子到日本實習一定能對她成為室內設計師非常有幫助，可知成為室內設計師應該是她的夢想。至於其他的選項，她要去的是日本，下個月去，而並沒有提到她喜不喜歡泰國菜，所以只能選(A)了。

---

2. 男子與女子為什麼這麼興奮？

    (A) 女子要出國唸書了。

    (B) 女子拿到想要的實習機會了。

    (C) 男子要出國唸書了。

    (D) 男子拿到想要的實習機會了。

女子一開始是說她得到了實習機會，可以去日本，兩人才會這麼開心。需要小心的是，一開始如果恍神掉了，沒聽到女子要去實習，會發現對話剩餘的內容就算女子其實是要去留學也說得通，所以聽題目時一定要非常小心，盡量不要錯失任何一句資訊。

3. 如果這個對話要下個標題，哪個比較好呢？

(A) 好消息。

(B) 美食。

(C) 室內設計小撇步。

(D) 把它炸開。

整個對話圍繞著女子的好消息打轉，可知標題應該就是「好消息」比較合適。女子提到的「it will be a blast」，指的是「會很好玩」的意思，但blast這個單字只在此片語中帶有「好玩的事」的意思，平常則作為「炸」的意思使用。在這裡當然不能選「把它炸開」這個選項了。

多益聽力搶分有祕密，全真模擬試題46

1. Where was the man this morning?　　🎧 **Track 46**

   (A) Outside the company.

   (B) In the office.

   (C) At a meeting.

   (D) In the basement.

2. Why was the woman unhappy at the man?

   (A) They couldn't find him in the morning.

   (B) He was late to the meeting.

   (C) He was hiding inside the basement.

   (D) He went out of the company.

3. Why did the woman forgive the man?

   (A) He fixed her computer.

   (B) He was nice to kittens.

   (C) He gave her sweets.

   (D) He brought her food.

GO ON TO THE NEXT PAGE

多益聽力搶分有祕密，
全真模擬試題-P195頁答案與詳解

題目解答

1. (D)   2. (A)   3. (B)

聽力原文

W: Why were you out of your office this morning? We wanted to discuss next month's budget but couldn't get hold of you. I'm not happy about this at all.

M: Sorry. I didn't leave the company building actually. I was in the basement.

W: The basement? What on earth were you doing there^澳?

M: Fixing a leak. And then I found two kittens living down there so I got them food.

W: Aw, so sweet! Okay, I forgive you.

搶分重點　❶ 口音為英國（男）與澳洲（女）。
　　　　　　❷ 澳洲腔的「there」念法和美國腔不同，仔細聽聽看！

聽力中譯

W：你今天早上怎麼沒在辦公室？我們想討論下個月的預算，但一直找不到你。我很不高興。

M：抱歉。我其實沒有離開公司大樓，而是在地下室。

W：地下室？你在那裡幹什麼？

M：修漏水。然後我發現兩隻小貓住在那裡，所以我幫牠們帶了食物。

W：唉呀，你人真好！好吧，我原諒你。

聽力題目詳解

1. 男子今天早上在哪裡？

   (A) 公司外面。

   (B) 辦公室裡。

   (C) 在開會。

   (D) 地下室。

多益聽力搶分有祕密，滿分高手10秒解題關鍵

有時候對話中的角色會自己替我們問我們需要知道的問題，如這題
的女子一開始就質問男子「早上在哪裡」，我們正好就知道男子的
答案將是這題的答案，而選出(D)。

2. 女子為什麼對男子不高興？

   (A) 他們早上找不到他。

   (B) 他開會遲到。

   (C) 他躲在地下室。

   (D) 他到公司外面去。

多益聽力搶分有祕密，滿分高手10秒解題關鍵

一群人要討論要事的時候有人不在，的確是個有點討厭的問題，因
此女子才會有點生男子的氣。男子雖然在地下室，但他並非刻意
「躲在」地下室，故意要大家找不到他，所以(C)選項不正確。

3. 女子為什麼原諒了男子？

(A) 他幫她修電腦。

(B) 他對小貓很好。

(C) 他給她糖果。

(D) 他帶食物給她。

多益聽力搶分有祕密，滿分高手10秒解題關鍵

女子稱讚男子「so sweet」，這裡的sweet是形容詞，是「人很好」的意思；而題目(C)選項中的sweets是名詞，指的是「糖果」的意思，這兩個sweet完全沒有關係，別被誤導了。

多益聽力搶分有祕密，全真模擬試題47

1. What are the man and woman discussing?　　🎧 **Track 47**

   (A) The company party.

   (B) The company competition.

   (C) The company dinner.

   (D) The company outing.

2. Why does the woman think karaoke is not a good choice?

   (A) It's too expensive.

   (B) They can't talk much.

   (C) She can't sing.

   (D) It's too far away.

3. Why does the woman think the others won't want to go to the beach?

   (A) Not a lot of them are outdoor people.

   (B) They prefer restaurants.

   (C) They don't like hot weather.

   (D) They can't swim.

GO ON TO THE NEXT PAGE

多益聽力搶分有祕密，
全真模擬試題-P199頁答案與詳解

題目解答

1. (D)　　　　2. (B)　　　　3. (A)

聽力原文

W: Where do you want to go for the company outing? I prefer the beach, but I guess not a lot of us are outdoor people.

M: Yeah, I think some of the younger guys would want to go to a movie instead. But what's the point of a company outing if no one talks to each other?

W: I know! Someone also suggested karaoke[2], but you can't talk much when karaokeing either; there's too much noise.

M: Maybe we should just pick a nice restaurant and have tea!

> **搶分重點**
>
> ❶ 口音為英國（男）與澳洲（女）。
> ❷ 「karaoke」這個字，我們會唸「卡拉OK」。但在英文中，一般母語人士碰到外來語的單字，常會直接以自然發音法的直覺去念它，所以他們念的方法就會和我們所熟知的「卡拉OK」不同，可以特別注意。

聽力中譯

W：你覺得公司出遊要去哪？我比較想去海邊，但大家感覺好像都不是很愛室外活動。

M：對啊，我想有些年輕男生會比較想去看電影。不過公司出遊都沒人講話，還有什麼意義啊？

W：我知道啊！也有人提議要去唱卡拉OK，可是卡拉OK也不能講
話啊，太吵了。

M：我們說不定應該挑一家不錯的餐廳喝喝茶就好了！

聽力題目詳解

1. 男子和女子在討論什麼？

(A) 公司派對。

(B) 公司競賽。

(C) 公司晚餐。

(D) 公司出遊。

多益聽力搶分有祕密，滿分高手10秒解題關鍵

女子一開始就提到了「公司出遊」（company outing），但就算漏
聽了，從兩人講到電影、卡拉OK、海邊等等選項，也可知他們討
論的不太可能會是晚餐或競賽。

2. 為什麼女子認為卡拉OK不是個好主意？

(A) 太貴了。

(B) 不方便講話。

(C) 她不會唱歌。

(D) 太遠了。

男子認為看電影的缺點就是不能好好聊天，而女子也同意，還說卡拉OK也是一樣，可見她認為不該去卡拉OK的原因應該就是「不方便講話」。

---

3. 為什麼女子認為其他人不會想去海邊？

(A) 他們多半不喜歡室外活動。

(B) 他們比較喜歡去餐廳。

(C) 他們不喜歡熱天氣。

(D) 他們不會游泳。

女子沒有提到天氣、餐廳和游泳的事，倒是說他們公司很少是「outdoor people」（直譯是「室外人」，就是指喜歡在室外的人），因此我們可以刪去不對的選項，而選擇(A)。

多益聽力搶分有祕密，全真模擬試題48

1. Who took the woman's stapler?   🎧 **Track 48**

   (A) The man.

   (B) The woman herself.

   (C) The man and woman's colleague.

   (D) We do not know.

2. Why did the woman ask the man about her stapler?

   (A) He sits in front of her office.

   (B) He works in her office.

   (C) He has a lot of staplers.

   (D) He likes to steal.

3. Which of the statements are true?

   (A) The man has been in the woman's office today.

   (B) The man is busy working today.

   (C) The man saw someone go into the woman's office today.

   (D) The woman saw the man go into her office today.

多益聽力搶分有祕密，
全真模擬試題-P203頁答案與詳解

題目解答

1. (D)　　　　2. (A)　　　　3. (B)

聽力原文

W: Someone took the stapler I left on my desk. Did you see anyone go in my office?

M: Huh? No. Even if someone did, I would be too busy with my work to notice.

W: Well, you sit right in front of my office, so if no one went in, you must be the culprit.

M: Hey, why would I want to steal a useless stapler? Besides, I never stepped into your office today at all.

> **搶分重點** 🔊 口音為英國（男）與澳洲（女）。

聽力中譯

W： 有人拿了我放在桌上的釘書機。你有看到有人進我辦公室嗎？

M： 啊？沒有。就算有人進去，我這麼忙，根本不會注意到。

W： 嗯，你就坐在我辦公室前面，所以如果沒人進去，你就是犯人了。

M： 喂，我幹嘛偷一個沒用的釘書機啊？而且我今天根本沒有踏進妳的辦公室啊。

聽力題目詳解

1. 誰拿了女子的釘書機？

(A) 男子。

(B) 女子自己拿的。

(C) 男子與女子的同事。

(D) 我們不知道。

多益聽力搶分有祕密，滿分高手10秒解題關鍵

現在整個呈現一種羅生門的狀況：可能是女子自己把釘書機收起來忘記了，可能是有同事走進女子的辦公室，男子卻沒看到……各種情況都有可能。因此，我們也只能選(D)，「不知道」了。

2. 女子為什麼問男子關於她釘書機的事？

(A) 他坐在她的辦公室前面。

(B) 他在她的辦公室裡工作。

(C) 他有很多釘書機。

(D) 他喜歡偷東西。

多益聽力搶分有祕密，滿分高手10秒解題關鍵

東西不見理論上應該還有其他人可以問，為什麼女子獨獨要問男子一人呢？女子提到男子坐在她的辦公室前面，而用常理推斷，無論是誰進女子的辦公室，坐在前面的男子都應該要看得一清二楚才對，因此女子才找他質問。答案選(A)。

3. 以下哪段話為真？

(A) 男子今天有進去過女子的辦公室。

(B) 男子今天很忙碌地在工作。

(C) 男子有看到有人進女子的辦公室。

(D) 女子今天有看到男子進她的辦公室。

多益聽力搶分有祕密，滿分高手10秒解題關鍵

男子自己坦承，自己並沒有進去女子的辦公室，而因為他很忙，所以也沒注意到有沒有人進女子的辦公室。因此，以男子沒有說謊為前提，可以判斷這四項中只有(B)是真的。那如果男子說謊呢？在考聽力測驗時不需要考慮這個問題，當作大家都是講真話即可。

多益聽力搶分有祕密，全真模擬試題49

1. Where are the man and the woman? 🎧 **Track 49**

   (A) On a train.

   (B) On a taxi.

   (C) On the subway.

   (D) On the bus.

2. Why did the conversation end?

   (A) The woman has to get off.

   (B) The man has to get off.

   (C) The woman caught a thief.

   (D) Something exciting happened.

3. What did the woman do yesterday?

   (A) She caught a customer stealing.

   (B) She filed papers.

   (C) She talked to the man.

   (D) She ran into the man.

GO ON TO THE NEXT PAGE

多益聽力搶分有祕密，
全真模擬試題-P207頁答案與詳解

題目解答

1. (D)   2. (B)   3. (A)

聽力原文

W: Hey, fancy running into you on the bus! It's been a long time since we talked. What have you been up to?

M: Same old boring life. I've been filing papers all day today. What about you?

W: I caught a customer stealing red-handed yesterday, but that's the first exciting thing that has happened this month.

M: Wow, our lives sure need some spicing-up. Gotta get off now; talk to you later^英!

> **搶分重點**
> ❶ 口音為英國（男）與澳洲（女）。
> ❷ 英國腔的「later」發音方式比較特別，和美國腔完全不同。

聽力中譯

W： 嘿，在公車上遇到你真巧啊！我們上次聊已經是很久以前了，你最近如何？

M： 生活一樣無聊啊，我整天都在整理文件。妳呢？

W： 我昨天當場逮到一個在偷東西的顧客，但這已經是這個月發生的第一件刺激的事了。

M： 哇，我們的人生真需要一點刺激啊。我要下車了，之後再聊啊！

聽力題目詳解

1. 男子和女子在哪裡？

    (A) 火車上。

    (B) 計程車上。

    (C) 地鐵上。

    (D) 公車上。

多益聽力搶分有祕密，滿分高手10秒解題關鍵

女子一開始說：「在公車上遇到你，真巧」（fancy running into you on the bus），可知兩人應該是在公車上碰到而開始對話，對話是在公車上發生的。

---

2. 這個對話為什麼會結束？

    (A) 女子要下車了。

    (B) 男子要下車了。

    (C) 女子逮到小偷了。

    (D) 發生了刺激的事。

多益聽力搶分有祕密，滿分高手10秒解題關鍵

最後對話結束，是因為男子說「要下車了，以後再聊」（Gotta get off now; talk to you later），而匆匆離開，所以選(B)。

3. 女子昨天做了什麼？

(A) 逮到顧客偷東西。

(B) 整理文件。

(C) 和男子說話。

(D) 遇到男子。

多益聽力搶分有祕密，滿分高手10秒解題關鍵

遇到男子、和男子說話都是今天（現在）在發生的事，而整理文件則是男子的工作女子說逮到顧客偷東西，所以她的工作可能和顧店比較有關，而不是整理文件。因此，女子昨天做的事只有可能是(A)。

多益聽力搶分有祕密，全真模擬試題50

1. Why did the woman become thinner?　　　　🎧 **Track 50**

(A) She has a secret.

(B) She went on a diet.

(C) She gave birth.

(D) She worked very hard.

2. What do we know about the woman?

(A) She gave birth to a son.

(B) She did not rest for long after giving birth.

(C) She did not pay attention to her coworkers.

(D) She gave birth last month.

3. What do we know about the man?

(A) He gave birth last week.

(B) He looks slimmer these days.

(C) He did not think giving birth was a big deal.

(D) He didn't pay attention to his coworkers much.

GO ON TO THE NEXT PAGE ➡

多益聽力搶分有祕密，
全真模擬試題-P211頁答案與詳解

題目解答

1. **(C)**　　　　　2. **(B)**　　　　　3. **(D)**

聽力原文

M: Hey, you look so much slimmer these days. What's the secret?

W: Uh, you really don't pay much attention to your coworkers, do you? I was pregnant and gave birth last week. Of course I would look thinner.

M: What? You gave birth last week and are already back at work?

W: I came back to work the day after I gave birth. It's not a big deal.

M: That's amazing; I could never do that.

搶分重點　🔊 口音為英國（男）與澳洲（女）。

聽力中譯

M：嘿，妳最近看起來瘦多了。有什麼秘訣啊？

W：呃，你實在不是很注意自己的同事，對不對？我之前懷孕，上禮拜生了，當然會看起來比較瘦啊。

M：什麼？妳上禮拜才生的，現在已經回來上班了？

W：我生完那天就回來了，根本沒什麼。

M：這太驚人了，我一定做不到。

聽力題目詳解

1. 女子為什麼變瘦了？

(A) 她有個祕密。

(B) 她減肥了。

(C) 她生了。

(D) 她很努力工作。

多益聽力搶分有祕密，滿分高手10秒解題關鍵

女子上個禮拜生完孩子，也難怪看起來會比較瘦。雖然她的確也很努力工作（一生完第二天就急呼呼地跑回去上班了），但這不是她變瘦的原因，應選(C)。

2. 關於女子，我們知道什麼事？

(A) 她生了兒子。

(B) 她生完沒有休息很久。

(C) 她不是很注意她的同事。

(D) 她上個月生完了。

多益聽力搶分有祕密，滿分高手10秒解題關鍵

女子上個禮拜生完以後，第二天就立刻若無其事地回去上班了，可知她生完沒有休息很久，應選(B)。

3. 關於男子，我們知道什麼事？

   (A) 他上個禮拜生了。

   (B) 他最近看起來比較瘦，

   (C) 他不覺得生產是什麼大事。

   (D) 他不太注意自己的同事。

多益聽力搶分有祕密，滿分高手10秒解題關鍵

同事已經懷胎十個月，還生了，卻完全沒發覺，同事上個禮拜有沒有來上班，他也沒發覺，可知男子應該很少在關心同事發生了什麼事，所以選(D)。目前的科技男子還不太可能生產，所以(A)的選項可以依常理直接剔除。

多益聽力搶分有祕密，全真模擬試題51

1. What is this conversation most likely about?　　🎧 **Track 51**

(A) A man is inviting his wife to a banquet.

(B) A high school student is inviting his friend to a party.

(C) A woman is inviting her husband to a gathering.

(D) A guy is inviting his girlfriend to a dance.

2. Who is Jodie most likely to be?

(A) She is likely the man and woman's colleague.

(B) She is likely the man and woman's child.

(C) She likely babysits for the man and woman sometimes.

(D) She is likely a professional dancer.

3. Will the woman accept the man's invitation?

(A) Not unless she finds someone to babysit the kids.

(B) No, because she has dance lessons.

(C) Yes, as long as it ends on time.

(D) Yes, as long as it is on Friday.

GO ON TO THE NEXT PAGE ➤

多益聽力搶分有祕密，
全真模擬試題-P215頁答案與詳解

題目解答

1. (A)   2. (C)   3. (A)

聽力原文

M: Are you coming to my company's end-of-year banquet with me?

W: When will it be?

M: Next Friday night. It starts at seven, and is supposed to end at nine but you know people never end those things on time.

W: Friday night? I guess I can't go. Who's going to look after the kids?

M: Can't we get Jodie to babysit? Oh, yeah, I remember now. Friday is when Jodie has dance lessons.

搶分重點　🔊 口音為英國（男）與澳洲（女）。
　　　　　　🔊 英國腔的「dance」發音方式和美國腔不同。

聽力中譯

M： 妳要來參加我們公司的年末晚宴嗎？

W： 什麼時候？

M： 下禮拜五晚上，七點開始，九點應該要結束，不過妳也知道這種活動哪有人會準時結束的。

W： 禮拜五晚上？我想我不能去，不然誰照顧孩子？

M： 不能找裘蒂來顧小孩嗎？喔對，我想起來了，禮拜五裘蒂要上舞蹈課。

聽力題目詳解

1. 這個對話很可能是關於什麼？

    (A) 一名男子在邀請太太去參加晚宴。

    (B) 一名高中生在邀請朋友去派對。

    (C) 一名女子在邀請先生去聚會。

    (D) 一名男子在邀請女友去舞會。

多益聽力搶分有祕密，滿分高手10秒解題關鍵

在考聽力測驗時，邊聽邊想像整個情境是很重要的。這個對話中雖然兩人沒有提到彼此間的關係，但從他們談論小孩的事和一些共同認識的人（例如由兩人沒有特別講裘蒂是誰，可以看出兩人都認識裘蒂）這幾點看來，我們可以依稀想像兩人應該很熟、而且還要一起為小孩的事煩惱，因此應該是夫妻最為合理。接下來再過濾掉(C)選項（是男子邀請女子，不是女子邀請男子），就可以選出正確答案(A)了。

---

2. 裘蒂很可能是誰？

    (A) 可能是男子與女子的同事。

    (B) 可能是男子與女子的孩子。

    (C) 可能有時候會幫男子與女子看顧小孩。

    (D) 可能是個職業舞者。

3. 女子會接受男子的邀請嗎？

(A) 除非她找到人幫忙看小孩，不然不會。

(B) 不會，因為她要上舞蹈課。

(C) 只要準時結束，就會。

(D) 只要是在禮拜五，就會。

多益聽力搶分有祕密，全真模擬試題52

1. Why does the woman have to leave?　　🎧 **Track 52**

(A) Her son is hurt.

(B) Her son got bad grades at school.

(C) She has to see a parent of her son's classmate.

(D) She has to buy a pen for her son.

2. What is true about the woman?

(A) She asked for the day off.

(B) She promised to be back for the meeting.

(C) She wants the man to talk to the parent.

(D) She promised to bring her son a pen.

3. What is true about the woman's son?

(A) He got in an accident.

(B) He hurt his teacher.

(C) He poked a classmate with a pen.

(D) He didn't go to school.

GO ON TO THE NEXT PAGE ▶

多益聽力搶分有祕密，
全真模擬試題-P219頁答案與詳解

題目解答

1. (C)   2. (B)   3. (C)

聽力原文

W: Sorry, Mr. Qin, I have to head to my son's school right now, but I promise I'll make it back before the meeting with the shareholders.

M: Why? Did something happen to him? Is he all right?

W: Oh, he's fine; he just poked a classmate with a pen and now the parent is demanding^澳 to see me.

M: Wow, that sounds like quite a hassle.

搶分重點　❶ 口音為英國（男）與澳洲（女）。
❷ 澳洲腔的「demand」念法和美國腔很不一樣。

聽力中譯

W：秦先生，不好意思，我現在得馬上去我兒子的學校，不過我保證我會在跟股份持有人開會前趕回來。

M：為什麼？發生了什麼事嗎？他還好嗎？

W：喔，他很好，他只是拿筆戳了同學，現在對方家長嚷著要件見我。

M：哇，這聽起來真麻煩。

聽力題目詳解

1. 為什麼女子要離開？

    (A) 她的兒子受傷了。

    (B) 她的兒子在學校成績不好。

    (C) 她得去見兒子同學的家長。

    (D) 她得為兒子買一枝筆。

多益聽力搶分有祕密，滿分高手10秒解題關鍵

女子說她的兒子一切安好，只是同學家長嚷著要見她，所以她只好去了，可知答案應該是(C)。雖然對話中確實提到了pen這個字，但筆是她兒子拿來戳同學用的東西，女子並不需要再幫他買一枝。

---

2. 關於女子，何者為真？

    (A) 她請一天假。

    (B) 她答應回來開會。

    (C) 她要男子去跟家長講話。

    (D) 她答應要帶一枝筆給兒子。

多益聽力搶分有祕密，滿分高手10秒解題關鍵

女子雖然和老闆請假，但她並不是要請一天的假，而是答應待會還會回來開會，可知不能選(A)，(B)才是正確答案。

3. 關於女子的兒子，何者為真？

   (A) 他出了意外。

   (B) 他傷到了老師。

   (C) 他用筆戳到同學。

   (D) 他沒去上學。

多益聽力搶分有祕密，滿分高手10秒解題關鍵

女子是因為兒子在學校闖禍而去學校，而非兒子出意外。此外，整個對話也沒有出現過teacher這個字，可見兒子闖的禍和老師無關，答案要選(C)。

多益聽力搶分有祕密，全真模擬試題53

1. Why is the man smoking in a non-smoking area?

   (A) He is deliberately violating the rules.　　**🎧 Track 53**

   (B) He misread a sign.

   (C) He didn't see any sign.

   (D) The woman told him to.

2. Where should the man go if he wants to smoke?

   (A) To where the man in orange is sitting.

   (B) To where the woman is sitting.

   (C) To the restrooms.

   (D) Stay right where he is.

3. What is the man's complaint?

   (A) That he should be able to smoke anywhere.

   (B) That the signs should be made clearer.

   (C) That he didn't like the man in orange.

   (D) That he didn't want to smoke.

GO ON TO THE NEXT PAGE ➡

多益聽力搶分有祕密，
全真模擬試題-P223頁答案與詳解

題目解答

1. (B)   2. (A)   3. (B)

....

聽力原文

W: I'm sorry, but you're not allowed to smoke here.

M: But I'm pretty sure I saw a sign that said "smoking area".

W: Yes, but it means the area over there—see where the man in orange is sitting? It's that area. If you want to smoke, then you'll have to head over there.

M: Okay. You people should make your signs clearer; I honestly thought^英 this was a smoking area. Sorry about that!

搶分重點　🔊 口音為英國（男）與澳洲（女）。
　　　　　　　🔊 英國腔的「thought」念法和美國腔不大一樣。

聽力中譯

W： 不好意思，您不能在這裡抽菸。

M： 可是我很確定我看到牌子寫「吸菸區」耶。

W： 對，可是那指的是那邊那個區域。你看到那個穿橘色的男人坐的地方了嗎？就是那一區。如果你想吸菸，你就要過去那一區。

M：好。你們應該要把牌子弄清楚點嘛，我真的以為這裡是吸菸區。抱歉啦！

聽力題目詳解

1. 男子為什麼在非吸菸區吸菸？

   (A) 他故意違反規則。

   (B) 他誤解牌子了。

   (C) 他沒有看到牌子。

   (D) 女子叫他這麼做的。

多益聽力搶分有祕密，滿分高手10秒解題關鍵

女子叫男子不要抽菸時，男子並沒有表現出一副「我就是想要啊」的不屑模樣，而是驚訝地說「這裡不是吸菸區嗎？牌子有寫啊」，可見他並非故意要違反規則，而純粹是看錯了牌子的意思，因此選 (B)。

---

2. 男子如果想吸菸，應該去哪裡？

   (A) 去穿橘色的男子坐的地方。

   (B) 去女子坐的地方。

   (C) 去洗手間。

   (D) 待在他原本所在的地方。

3. 男子抱怨什麼？

    (A) 他應該要在哪裡都能吸菸才對。

    (B) 牌子應該要清楚點。

    (C) 他不喜歡穿橘色的男子。

    (D) 他不想吸菸。

多益聽力搶分有祕密，全真模擬試題54

1. Who is the man most likely to be? 🎧 **Track 54**

   (A) The woman's professor.

   (B) The woman's husband.

   (C) The woman's landlord.

   (D) The woman's friend.

2. Which of these animals is allowed in this apartment?

   (A) A giraffe.

   (B) A hamster.

   (C) A sheepdog.

   (D) A pony.

3. Why is the woman not allowed to keep chickens?

   (A) They are too large.

   (B) They might be noisy.

   (C) They are dirty and smelly.

   (D) The neighbors are allergic.

GO ON TO THE NEXT PAGE

題目解答

1. (C)   2. (B)   3. (B)

聽力原文

W: Am I allowed to keep a pet when living in this apartment?

M: It depends on the pet. Fish and small reptiles or rodents should be all right, but dogs might disturb the other tenants. Larger animals like horses are of course [2] out of the question, since they won't fit.

W: What about chickens?

M: Chickens? Sorry, but no. If your rooster crows in the early morning, I may get complaints from your neighbors.

搶分重點

- [1] 口音為英國（男）與澳洲（女）。
- [2] 男子在「of course」兩字特別加了重音，是因為想強調套房裡「當然」不能養馬。我們可以想像兩人對話的場景或許是狹小的套房，男子正指著房間裡所剩無幾的空間和女子說明「當然」裝不下馬。

聽力中譯

W： 我住這間套房的時候可以養寵物嗎？

M： 要看是什麼寵物。魚啦、小的爬蟲類或囓齒類動物就沒關係，可是狗可能會打擾到其他承租人。大一點的動物，像馬之類的，當然就不可能了，因為塞不下。

W： 那雞呢？

M： 雞喔？抱歉，不行。如果妳的公雞一早就啼叫，妳的鄰居可能
會來找我抗議。

聽力題目詳解

1. 男子很可能是誰？

  (A) 女子的教授。

  (B) 女子的丈夫。

  (C) 女子的房東。

  (D) 女子的朋友。

多益聽力搶分有祕密，滿分高手10秒解題關鍵

從對話中的apartment（套房）與tenant（承租人）等關鍵字，或
許就可以判斷這個對話和租屋有關。就算沒有聽懂這兩個單字，也
可從女子問男子可不可以在這裡養寵物這件事判斷。一般是不會問
教授可不可以養寵物的，而對丈夫或朋友用「allow（允許）」這
個字又很奇怪，因為和親密的人說話好像不需要這麼低聲下氣，可
知要選(C)。

2. 可以在這個套房養下列哪隻動物？

  (A) 長頸鹿。

  (B) 倉鼠。

  (C) 牧羊犬。

  (D) 小馬。

房東先生說馬一類比較大的動物會養不下，可知(D)並非正確選項，而(A)長頸鹿還比馬更高，可見也不能選。雖然牧羊犬是乖乖的狗，但房東擔心狗叫會吵人，所以(C)也不允許，只能選又小又安靜的倉鼠了。

3. 女子為什麼不能養雞？

    (A) 太大了。

    (B) 太吵了。

    (C) 又髒又臭。

    (D) 鄰居會過敏。

男子說女子的雞如果一早啼叫會引來鄰居抗議，可知他認為雞會吵人，要選(B)。雖然他的確也提到雞會對鄰居造成影響，但並非因為牠會讓鄰居「過敏」，可知(D)並非正確選項。

多益聽力搶分有祕密，全真模擬試題55

1. Why does the man not want to go to dance class?

    (A) He can't dance.   🎧 **Track 55**

    (B) He thinks it's boring.

    (C) He is too busy.

    (D) He doesn't like the teacher.

2. Why is the man unable to make it to class at eight?

    (A) He will be on a business trip.

    (B) He will be sleeping.

    (C) He will be working late.

    (D) He will be doing an operation.

3. What will the man be doing tomorrow?

    (A) He will be on a business trip.

    (B) He will be dancing.

    (C) He will be going over material.

    (D) He will be working late.

GO ON TO THE NEXT PAGE ➤

多益聽力搶分有祕密，
全真模擬試題-P231頁答案與詳解

題目解答

1. (C)   2. (C)   3. (A)

聽力原文

W: Why don't you take dance classes with me? We get a discount if we sign up together.

M: Sorry. I'm juggling three jobs and operating on barely^英 enough sleep, so I don't have time for that.

W: That's nonsense! There is always time to dance. You should come to the next session tonight at eight.

M: I won't be able to make it. I'm going on a business trip tomorrow and will probably be working late to go over some material with my supervisor.

> **搶分重點**　　🔊 口音為英國（男）與澳洲（女）。
> 　　　　　　　🔊 英國腔的「barely」念法和美國腔不太一樣。

聽力中譯

W：你為什麼不跟我去上跳舞課呢？一起報名會有打折耶。

M：抱歉啦，我同時有三個工作，幾乎都睡眠不足了，沒時間啦。

W：亂講一通！再怎麼忙，都會有時間跳舞的。你今天晚上八點應該來上下一期的課。

M：我去不了，我明天要出差，大概會加班很晚，和我的主管討論一些資料。

聽力題目詳解

1. 男子為什麼不想去上舞蹈課？

　　(A) 他不會跳舞。

　　(B) 他覺得很無聊。

　　(C) 他太忙了。

　　(D) 他不喜歡老師。

多益聽力搶分有祕密，滿分高手10秒解題關鍵

男子說他一共有三個工作，都已經睡眠不足了，哪有空去跳舞，可見他不去上舞蹈課的理由是因為太忙。他並沒有提到他喜不喜歡跳舞、或喜不喜歡老師，甚至從頭到尾根本沒講到跳舞的事，可見其他三個選項都不可選。

---

2. 男子為什麼無法八點去上課？

　　(A) 他要出差。

　　(B) 他在睡覺。

　　(C) 他會加班很晚。

　　(D) 他要動手術。

男子是因為隔天要出差，晚上必須加班準備，才無法去上課。出差是隔天的事情，並非當晚就出差，所以不可選(A)。此外，男子在對話中說的「operate」指的是「運作」，他想表達的是「我靠著很少的睡眠時間，還是能運作」的意思。這和題目選項(D)中代表「手術」的operation意思完全不同。

3. 男子明天會做什麼？

   (A) 出差。

   (B) 跳舞。

   (C) 討論資料。

   (D) 加班。

男子之所以晚上要加班討論資料，就是因為第二天要出差，可見「明天」要做的事是「出差」。「討論資料」和「加班」都是「今天晚上」要做的事，所以不能選，而男子根本沒把「跳舞」放在眼裡，所以也非正確的選項。

多益聽力搶分有祕密，全真模擬試題56

1. Why does the woman look tired?　　　🎧 **Track 56**

   (A) She worked especially hard yesterday.

   (B) She had been losing sleep.

   (C) She was too worried about the man.

   (D) She forgot to put on makeup.

2. What does the man suggest the woman do?

   (A) Put on more makeup.

   (B) Get some rest.

   (C) See a doctor.

   (D) Get some better eyeliner.

3. What makes the woman look tired?

   (A) Her bad skin.

   (B) Her red eyes.

   (C) The dark circles under her eyes.

   (D) Her slouching posture.

GO ON TO THE NEXT PAGE

多益聽力搶分有祕密，
全真模擬試題-P235頁答案與詳解

題目解答

1. (D)   2. (B)   3. (C)

聽力原文

M: You look quite exhausted today. Did anything happen?

W: I do? I'm feeling pretty normal.

M: Look in the mirror and see for yourself. Those dark circles under your eyes are frightening^英! I think you're overworking yourself.

W: Oh, wow! I do look horrible. But don't worry; I just forgot to put on makeup today.

M: So this is how you normally look? You should really get some rest.

> **搶分重點** **1** 口音為英國（男）與澳洲（女）。
> **2** 認真聽聽看「frightening」這個字的發音方式，是不是和字面上看起來的樣子不太一樣呢？

聽力中譯

M： 妳今天看起來真累。發生了什麼事嗎？

W： 會嗎？我感覺很正常啊。

M： 自己照鏡子就知道了。妳眼睛下面的黑眼圈太恐怖了！妳一定太操勞了。

W： 喔，哇賽，我看起來真的很糟。不過不用擔心，我只是今天忘記化妝。

M： 所以妳平常根本就長這樣？那妳真的該好好休息了。

聽力題目詳解

1. 女子為什麼看起來很累？

　　(A) 她昨天工作得特別努力。

　　(B) 她失眠。

　　(C) 她太為男子擔心了。

　　(D) 她忘記化妝了。

多益聽力搶分有祕密，滿分高手10秒解題關鍵

男子說女子看起來很累時，她沒有回答「是啊，昨天加班」等等理由，反而很驚訝地說「有嗎？」，可見她覺得自己很正常，並沒有特別做什麼辛苦的事。因此，(A)、(B)、(C)這些可以拿出來抱怨的事都可以剔除。女子後來拿起鏡子一看，馬上就知道原因是自己忘記化妝，可知要選(D)。

---

2. 男子建議女子做什麼？

　　(A) 化濃一點的妝。

　　(B) 多休息。

　　(C) 看醫生。

　　(D) 買更好的眼線。

男子認為女子看起來特別神情憔悴，一定是最近太累了，後來才知道原來她根本平常就都長這樣，依男子的邏輯來看，這不就代表她平常就太累了嗎？因此，也難怪男子會建議女子要多休息了。

3. 是什麼讓女子看起來很累？

   (A) 她糟糕的皮膚。

   (B) 她紅紅的眼睛。

   (C) 她的黑眼圈。

   (D) 她彎腰駝背的姿態。

一看到這題，就可以猜想到男子一定會評論女子的某個部分看起來很糟，而且一定是這四個中的一個。因此可以先暫時記住這四件事，一旦男子一講到，就可以馬上把答案寫下來，然後迅速忘記其他三個，別讓它們佔走你的「記憶體」。

多益聽力搶分有祕密，全真模擬試題57

1. What do we know about the woman?   🎧 **Track 57**

(A) She has already paid her taxes.

(B) This is her first time paying taxes.

(C) She is an expert in paying taxes.

(D) She bought software to help pay taxes.

2. Which of the following is true?

(A) The man has not paid his taxes.

(B) The deadline to pay taxes is next week.

(C) The man will pay taxes for the woman.

(D) The woman will figure out how to pay taxes in the night.

3. Why does the man tell the woman to hurry?

(A) The lunch break will be over soon.

(B) The deadline for tax filing is approaching soon.

(C) The software will soon be no longer downloadable.

(D) Paying taxes gets more difficult later.

GO ON TO THE NEXT PAGE ➡

多益聽力搶分有祕密，
全真模擬試題-P239頁答案與詳解

題目解答

1. (B)　　　　2. (B)　　　　3. (B)

聽力原文

M: Have you paid your taxes yet?

W: Not yet. I'm not even sure how to pay taxes since it's my first time.

M: It's actually quite easy. There's even downloadable software that can help you with it.

W: All right, I'll get to figuring it out at lunch break. The deadline for tax filing is next week, right?

M: Yes, so you'd better hurry.

> **搶分重點**　◀♪ 口音為英國（男）與澳洲（女）。

聽力中譯

M： 妳繳稅了沒？

W： 還沒耶。我連怎麼繳稅都不是很清楚，因為我今年第一次繳。

M： 其實蠻簡單的。甚至還有可下載的軟體能幫妳處理呢！

W： 好，那我午餐時間來研究一下。報稅的期限是下禮拜，對吧？

M： 是啊，所以妳最好快點。

聽力題目詳解

1. 關於女子，我們知道什麼？

(A) 她已經繳稅了。

(B) 這是她第一次繳稅。

(C) 她是繳稅專家。

(D) 她買了軟體來幫她繳稅。

多益聽力搶分有祕密，滿分高手10秒解題關鍵

(A)：男子一開始問她繳稅了沒時，女子說「還沒」，可知答案不會是(A)。(C)：女子說她甚至連怎麼繳稅都不太清楚，可知她絕對不會是專家。(D)：男子提到繳稅軟體的事，女子則說午休時會研究一下，可知她還沒有買任何軟體來幫忙。綜觀下來只能選(B)。

2. 下列何者為真？

(A) 男子沒繳稅。

(B) 繳稅的期限是下禮拜。

(C) 男子會替女子繳稅。

(D) 女子會在晚上搞懂怎麼繳稅。

(A)：男子問女子有沒有繳稅，但他並沒有提到他自己有沒有繳，所以我們無法確定，因此不選(A)。(C)：男子從來沒有答應過要幫女子繳稅。(D)：女子說要在「lunch break」時間研究繳稅的事。雖然各個工作場合吃「lunch」（午餐）的時間可能不同，但總之不會拖到晚上才吃午餐，可見這個答案也不對。因此要選(B)。

---

3. 男子為什麼叫女子快點？

    (A) 午休快結束了。

    (B) 報稅的期限快到了。

    (C) 軟體快不能下載了。

    (D) 繳稅越晚越難。

男子叫女子「hurry」，是接在女子問「報稅期限是下禮拜，對吧」之後，可知他是想提醒她報稅期限快到了，得趕快了。男子也沒有提到軟體的下載期限、午休的期限等，可知要選(B)。

多益聽力搶分有祕密，全真模擬試題58

1. What is NOT true about the woman?　　　🎧 **Track 58**

   (A) Her name is Jen.

   (B) She is in class now.

   (C) She is the man's client.

   (D) She takes yoga class.

2. Why did the man call the wrong person?

   (A) The person he was looking for and the person he called have the same number.

   (B) The person he was looking for and the person he called have the same name.

   (C) The person he was looking for and the person he called live together.

   (D) The person he was looking for and the person he called swapped phones.

3. What is the relation between the man and the woman?

   (A) They're in the same yoga class.

   (B) They live together.

   (C) They are business partners.

   (D) They share a phone.

GO ON TO THE NEXT PAGE ➡

多益聽力搶分有祕密，
全真模擬試題-P243頁答案與詳解

題目解答

1. (C)　　　　　2. (B)　　　　　3. (A)

聽力原文

M: Hi. Is this Jen?

W: Yes. Uh, Nick, why are you calling at this time of the day? You know I'm in class.

M: Oh, you're Jen from yoga class? I'm sorry! I thought you were someone else. I have a client named Jen too, you see. I wanted to ask her about a detail in our contract.

W: Well, just don't list all the Jens you know under the same name in your phone. That should solve the problem.

M: You're right, especially considering there are 4 Jens on my phone.

> **搶分重點** 🔊 口音為英國（男）與澳洲（女）。

聽力中譯

M：哈囉，是珍嗎？

W：對。呃，尼克，為什麼這個時候打來？你知道我在上課啊。

M：喔，妳是瑜伽課的珍嗎？抱歉！我以為妳是別人。我有個客戶也叫珍，我想問她我們合約的一個細節。

W：那就不要把所有你認識的珍都在手機裡取同一個名字啊，這樣就不會有問題了。

M：妳說得對，尤其我手機上就列了四個「珍」呢。

聽力題目詳解

1. 關於女子，何者不為真？

(A) 她的名字叫做珍。

(B) 她正在上課。

(C) 她是男子的客戶。

(D) 她有上瑜伽課。

多益聽力搶分有祕密，滿分高手10秒解題關鍵

男子想要找他的客戶，卻錯打到女子那裡去。女子並非他的客戶，
而是瑜伽課的同學，所以(C)選項不為真，要選(C)。

2. 男子為何打電話打錯人？

(A) 他要找的人和他打電話給她的那個人號碼一樣。

(B) 他要找的人和他打電話給她的那個人名字一樣。

(C) 他要找的人和他打電話給她的那個人住在一起。

(D) 他要找的人和他打電話給她的那個人交換了手機。

多益聽力搶分有祕密，滿分高手10秒解題關鍵

從對話中男子以「我有個客戶也叫珍」來向女子解釋可知，他會錯
打給女子是因為她的名字也和客戶一樣叫「珍」，所以選(B)。

3. 男子與女子是什麼關係？

(A) 他們一起上瑜伽課。

(B) 他們住在一起。

(C) 他們是工作伙伴。

(D) 他們共用手機。

多益聽力搶分有祕密，滿分高手10秒解題關鍵

由男子問「妳是瑜伽課的那個珍喔？」可知兩人是瑜伽課的同學，並非他想找的那個「珍」。答案要選(A)。

多益聽力搶分有祕密，全真模擬試題59

1. Why does the woman suggest that the man get another job? 🎧 **Track 59**

   (A) Packaging is too tiring for him.

   (B) He is not being paid well enough.

   (C) He is not a full-time employee yet.

   (D) His boss is giving him a raise.

2. What did the man's boss say regarding a raise?

   (A) That he will give the man a raise right now.

   (B) That he cannot give the man a raise now, but will later.

   (C) That he will never give the man a raise.

   (D) That he has already given the man a raise.

3. Why is the man upset?

   (A) He works full time, yet is paid less than a part-timer.

   (B) He thinks his boss likes the woman better.

   (C) The company might go broke.

   (D) The boss gave someone else a raise, but not him.

GO ON TO THE NEXT PAGE

多益聽力搶分有祕密，
全真模擬試題-P247頁答案與詳解

題目解答

1. (B)　　　　　2. (B)　　　　　3. (A)

聽力原文

M: I'm very unhappy about my current work situation. I mean, I'm a full-time employee, and yet I get paid less than the guy who helps us with packaging in the afternoons.

W: Really? That's a bit unfair. You should ask your boss for a raise.

M: Believe me, I tried. He told me that we're short of funds right now, but promised me that when things get better he will give me what I deserve.

W: That sounds like a ton of nonsense. I think you should consider looking for another position.

搶分重點
❶ 口音為英國（男）與澳洲（女）。
❷ 英國腔的「better」念法和我們習慣的美國腔不太一樣。

聽力中譯

M： 我現在工作的狀況讓我很不高興。我是說，我可是全職員工耶，可是我卻比每天下午來幫我們包裝貨物的那個人還領更少的錢。

W： 真的喔？這有點不公平。你應該跟老闆要求加薪。

M： 相信我，我有試過。他說我們現在資金短缺，但答應我等狀況好轉，他就會給我我應得的報酬。

W： 聽起來真是一堆屁話。我覺得你應該開始找別的職位了。

聽力題目詳解

1. 女子為什麼建議男子另找別的工作？

   (A) 包裝貨物對他來説太累了。

   (B) 他的薪水不夠好。

   (C) 他還不是全職員工。

   (D) 他老闆要給他加薪。

多益聽力搶分有祕密，滿分高手10秒解題關鍵

(A)：男子提到另一名員工是負責包裝貨物的，但並沒有説他自己的工作是什麼。既然我們不知道他的工作和包裝貨物是否有關，也無法確定包裝貨物對他來説累不累了，所以不能選(A)。(C)：男子一開始就説自己是全職員工，所以這個選項是不對的。(D)：老闆要加薪是好事，理論上女子不會因此勸他找別的工作。

---

2. 關於加薪的事，男子的老闆怎麼説？

   (A) 他現在就會給男子加薪。

   (B) 他現在不會給男子加薪，但之後會。

   (C) 他永遠不會給男子加薪。

   (D) 他已經給男子加薪過了。

3. 男子為什麼不高興？

　(A) 他全職工作，但錢卻比打工的還拿得少。

　(B) 他覺得他老闆比較喜歡女子。

　(C) 公司可能會破產。

　(D) 老闆給其他人加薪，卻沒給他加。

多益聽力搶分有祕密，全真模擬試題60

1. What is the woman likely in charge of?　　🎧 **Track 60**

　(A) Working in the factory.

　(B) Making products.

　(C) Introducing products.

　(D) Making calls.

2. What do we know about Ms. Oshima?

　(A) She is the woman's friend.

　(B) She works in the factory.

　(C) Her seat is by the door.

　(D) She is the woman's boss.

3. Why might the woman need to call the factory?

　(A) Some products might have problems.

　(B) She might have questions regarding some products.

　(C) She might need to meet customers there.

　(D) She might be working there when the man is in New York.

GO ON TO THE NEXT PAGE

多益聽力搶分有祕密，
全真模擬試題-P251頁答案與詳解

題目解答

1. (C)　　　　　　2. (C)　　　　　　3. (B)

聽力原文

M: We are going to attend an exhibition in New York next month. I expect you to be able to answer questions for prospective customers, so you should get familiar with our products within these few days.

W: I'll do my best. If I have a question regarding the products, who do I ask?

M: You'll have to call someone at the factory. You can get their number from Ms. Oshima, whose seat is there by the door.

W: I see. Thanks for the pointers; I'll get to work now.

> **搶分重點**
> ❶ 口音為英國（男）與澳洲（女）。
> ❷ 英國腔的「answer」念法和美國腔不太一樣。

聽力中譯

M：我們下個月要到紐約參展，我要妳回答可能合作的客戶問題，所以妳這幾天應該要熟悉一下我們的產品。

W：我會盡力。如果我對產品有疑問，我該問誰？

M：妳得打給工廠的人。妳可以跟坐門口的大島小姐要他們的電話。

W：瞭解了。謝謝你的提醒，我馬上開始工作。

聽力題目詳解

1. 女子的工作很可能是？

(A) 在工廠工作。

(B) 製作產品。

(C) 介紹產品。

(D) 打電話。

多益聽力搶分有祕密，滿分高手10秒解題關鍵

從兩人的對話聽起來，女子的工作有：參加展覽、回答顧客問題。
而男子說，如果女子有問題，她可以打給工廠的人，可見女子並非
在工廠工作，製作產品也不是她的分內事務。因此，可以猜想女子
應該是負責對外推銷產品的業務，因此選(C)。

---

2. 關於大島小姐，我們知道什麼？

(A) 她是女子的朋友。

(B) 她在工廠工作。

(C) 她坐在門口。

(D) 她是女子的老闆。

大島小姐到底是什麼身分，其實對話中沒有提到。我們只知道(1)如果女子想打給工廠的人，得和大島小姐要電話，(2)她坐在門口這兩件事，因此只要在四個選項中找提到這兩件事的選項，然後選出來就可以了，所以這題選(C)。

3. 女子為什麼可能需要打給工廠？

    (A) 有些產品可能有問題。

    (B) 她可能有和產品有關的問題。

    (C) 她可能需要在那裡見顧客。

    (D) 男子在紐約時，她可能會在那裡工作。

(A)與(B)兩個選項看起來似乎很類似，但其實「產品有問題」跟「有和產品相關的問題」完全是兩回事。(A)代表產品故障了、有瑕疵等等，而(B)代表女子對產品有不瞭解的地方。只要釐清兩者的差別就可以選出(B)。

原來如此 系列 *E150*

100%滿分命中奇蹟:
7天全面征服新多益聽力對話
最仿真的考題／最專業的解析

作　　者	張慈庭英語研發團隊
審　　定	金色證書編輯團隊
顧　　問	曾文旭
總 編 輯	王毓芳
編輯統籌	耿文國、黃璽宇
主　　編	吳靜宜、張辰安
執行編輯	林冠妤
美術編輯	王桂芳、王文璇
行銷企劃	姜怡安
特約編輯	汪瑩瑩
法律顧問	北辰著作權事務所　蕭雄淋律師、嚴裕欽律師

印　　製	世和印製企業有限公司
初　　版	2016年09月
出　　版	捷徑文化出版事業有限公司
電　　話	（02）2752-5618
傳　　真	（02）2752-5619
地　　址	106 台北市大安區忠孝東路四段250號11樓之1

定　　價	新台幣320元／港幣107元
產品內容	1書+1光碟

總 經 銷	采舍國際有限公司
地　　址	235 新北市中和區中山路二段366巷10號3樓
電　　話	（02）8245-8786
傳　　真	（02）8245-8718

港澳地區總經銷	和平圖書有限公司
地　　址	香港柴灣嘉業街12號百樂門大廈17樓
電　　話	（852）2804-6687
傳　　真	（852）2804-6409

🐾 **捷徑 Book站**　　書中圖片由Shutterstock網站提供。

現在就上臉書（FACEBOOK）「捷徑BOOK站」並按讚加入粉絲團，
就可享每月不定期新書資訊和粉絲專享小禮物喔！
http://www.facebook.com/royalroadbooks
讀者來函：royalroadbooks@gmail.com

本書如有缺頁、破損或倒裝，
請寄回捷徑文化出版社更換。
106 台北市大安區忠孝東路四段250號11樓之1
編輯部收

【版權所有　翻印必究】

國家圖書館出版品預行編目資料

100%滿分命中奇蹟: 7天全面征服新多益聽力對
話 / 張慈庭英語研發團隊著. -- 初版. -- 臺北市:
捷徑文化, 2016.09　面；　公分（原來如此:
E150）
ISBN 978-986-93561-1-4 (平裝附光碟)

1. 多益測驗

805.1895　　　　　　　　　　105015446